FIFTY DAYS TO DOOM

The galaxy is at war between the oxygen-breathing Terran Federation of worlds and the Ginzoes, chlorine-breathing aliens. An Earth ship is captured in battle by the Ginzoes, and its crew learns that the aliens have a newly developed catalyst. This can liberate chlorine from the sea — which, for the Ginzoes, would convert Terran worlds into suitable environments. The catalyst will be used unless the Terran Federation declares peace within fifty days. Fifty days to save Mankind . . . or fifty days to doom!

E. C. TUBB

FIFTY DAYS TO DOOM

Complete and Unabridged

LINFORD
Leicester

First published in Great Britain

First Linford Edition
published 2010

British Library CIP Data

Tubb, E. C.
    Fifty days to doom. - -
    (Linford mystery library)
    1. Space warfare– –Fiction. 2. Science fiction.
    3. Large type books.
    I. Title II. Series
    823.9′14–dc22

    ISBN 978–1–44480–189–7

Published by
F. A. Thorpe (Publishing)
Anstey, Leicestershire

Set by Words & Graphics Ltd.
Anstey, Leicestershire
Printed and bound in Great Britain by
T. J. International Ltd., Padstow, Cornwall

This book is printed on acid-free paper

1

Waiting to die

The ship stank. A queer, nose-biting combination of human and mechanical odours that only a ship in space can ever really know. An acrid odour, sickening, nasty, tasting flatly in the mouth and seeming to permeate into every nook and corner of the great vessel. A combination of seared flesh and burnt insulation, of dried blood and seeping chemicals, of acrid fumes and human sweat. Mingled with it, part of it, the taint of rotting food and stale air grew steadily stronger, dimming the sweet-bitter smell of liberated energy and joining with the mounting stench of human life which has wallowed in its own waste for too long.

It was a peculiar smell, the kind of smell that only a space ship can ever know, and then only in special conditions.

The smell of a ship that has been in violent combat — and lost.

Carl Ranson rubbed the thick stubble coating his chin and blinked red eyes as he peered through the candle-lit gloom. They were ridiculous, those candles, something from the dim and distant past, relics almost, something to be wondered at and even perhaps laughed at. But when all energy had been drained from a ship, when the emergency lights had faded and even the glo-plates remained dull through lack of free electrons to illuminate their treated surfaces with brilliant fluorescence, the lowly candle had its uses. They guttered now, dim in the oxygen-poor air, and their tiny flames seemed a mockery to the eyes of men used to the flaring radiance of normal lighting.

Handley grunted and settled back on his haunches, his broad features glistening in the dim light.

'Any good?' Ranson leaned forward, his eyes narrowing as he stared at the dismantled bulk of the generator. Handley shook his head.

'No. It would take a full sized workshop to get this thing working again. When they sucked the energy from us they ruined every electrical component in the ship.'

'I know that, but can't you rewire it? The pile is still operating, all we need is something to transform the atomic heat into usable current.'

'It took three hundred years for men to learn how to do that efficiently,' reminded the engineer wearily. 'It's no good, Carl. This ship's just so much junk now.' He stared at the young commander. 'What are we going to do?'

'What can we do?' Ranson closed his sore eyes and leaned against the once-bright surface of a bulkhead. 'When the Ginzoes caught us we'd just emerged from hyperspace. Conner saw them and fired the turret guns, for all the good he did he might as well have sprayed them with water. Two shots he fired, then they cut loose with their vortex guns.' He opened his eyes and stared at the engineer. 'I don't have to tell you what happened then.'

'They sucked the energy from us as if they were squeezing a water-filled sponge.' Handley swore as he kicked at the generator. 'The insulation went. The fuses blew and the ship died. I heard Conner scream, just one scream, then he was roasted by the free energy. I thought that I'd been blinded, then, when I opened my eyes I was sure of it. You'll never know how I felt when you came in here with a lighted candle.'

'Yes,' said Ranson, and his eyes were dull as he stared at the ruined generator. 'The ship died, all of it, and I wish that we had died at the same time.'

Handley grunted, not answering, and together they stared at the tangled ruin of what had once been an efficient machine.

'Three of us,' said Ranson quietly. 'Three left out of nine. Those vortex guns are very efficient.'

Again silence closed around them and in the deathly stillness the sounds of a man coughing echoed flatly against the smooth metal of the hull, The coughing seemed to go on for a long time, then, slowly and painfully, moving as a very old man might move, footsteps rang against the metal and a tall, thin figure entered the engine room.

He stood just within the door, blinking in the dim lighting his white hair a tangled mass over his high forehead. Age had stooped his shoulders and wrinkled his sere skin. Age had withered his hands and made his steps faulty, his bones brittle and his blood thin. But age had not dimmed the intelligence flaring in his pale, washed-out blue eyes. Against the broad figure of the engineer and the slender litheness of the commander he seemed almost a caricature of a man, a travesty of a human being, with pipe-stem arms and twig-like legs, and a disproportioned skull. He stood, the dim light reflecting from his pale eyes, and his voice echoed like the dry rustling of many bones.

'Well, Commander? When do we proceed?'

'We don't,' said Ranson shortly. 'This is the end of the journey.'

'Impossible!' Anger sharpened the dry whisper. 'I must get to Deneb IV. I should have been there by now. Is this the way you carry out your charter?'

'No.' Ranson felt too tired to feel anger. 'I accepted your charter with specific provisions as to enemy action. I am sorry Warren, but I'm afraid that you will never reach Deneb IV. I doubt very much whether you will ever reach anywhere ever again. Except Hell, of course, that is the only destination any of us can be certain of reaching.'

'Do not jest, young man!' Warren stared at the engineer. 'Well? Can't you do whatever it is that has to be done? Or are you as incompetent as your Captain?'

'I am human,' growled the engineer. 'This is one spot your money can't buy you out of, old man. This is the end of the line!'

'So you have failed.' The swollen head dipped a little as the financier stared at the young commander. 'You took my money under false pretences. You are nothing but a cheap crook!'

'Steady, old man!' Ranson straightened himself from the bulkhead and his pale cheeks flushed with red. 'I warned you what the dangers were before we left. I told you that if we were caught the Ginzoes would blast us. Well, we were caught, and they did blast us, and that's all there is to it.'

'Nonsense!' The old man didn't attempt

to hide his sneer. 'Everyone knows that you Free Traders have a working agreement with the enemy. In a way you're neutrals, that is why I chartered you, to get me safely to Deneb IV. I could have gone by passenger transport with greater comfort and less cost, but I was willing to pay for immunity. How is it that we were attacked?'

'We were attacked because we are Terrans.' Ranson slumped wearily against the bulkhead again, his heavy lids drooping over his grey eyes. 'What you don't seem to realise, Warren, you and most of the other people on the safe planets, is that we are at war. It is a funny kind of war, but war just the same. The Ginzoes don't want our planets, they couldn't use them if we gave them away, and neither could we use theirs. We are oxygen breathers, they are chlorine breathers, the atmosphere of each would kill the other. Neither side has any use whatever for the possessions of the other — and yet we are at war.'

'I know that, young man. But they started it first.'

'Does it matter?' Ranson shrugged. 'All I know is that it is one of the stupidest wars ever to be fought. We could blast their planets, of course, but then so could they ours. That was tried in the early days and twenty million people lost their lives on Altair alone. It didn't take long for the commanders to realise that planet-blasting was a double-edged weapon. They could do it — but they got back twice what they laid out, and now the war is fought strictly in space.'

'So?'

'So we were in space and they fired on us.'

'But didn't you shoot at them?'

'Naturally, but this is a small vessel with only one turret. They had a warship carrying vortex guns. A cruiser might have been able to give them battle — we couldn't.'

Ranson sighed as he leaned, almost unconscious from exhaustion, against the bulkhead.

'You made a mistake in your destination, Warren,' he said. 'Deneb IV is an oxygen planet surrounded by three chlorine planets. The Ginzoes want us to move away from the area, just as we want them to move out of the Centaurian System. There we have five O planets against their two C ones. Both sides are trying to get complete dominance over their own areas, they just don't like us near them and, for the same reason we don't want them near us. Don't ask me why, personally, I can't see why we just don't share the planets between us and forget this senseless war, but then, I'm just a space rat and I wouldn't understand the intricacies of strategy.'

Warren grunted, his pale eyes glittering as he stared about the dimness of the engine room.

'Then why did they fire on us? We were doing no harm.'

'We were heading towards Deneb IV. They always fire on any ship approaching a C-predominant area. We do the same of course. Any Ginzo ship heading towards an O-predominant area is fair game. They want us to get out from Deneb IV, and so they allow outgoing ships free passage. We do the same.' Ranson laughed, a short bark of sound utterly without humour. 'They call it war! It is, of course, a gentleman's war, with each side following strict rules of conduct. Not because they want to, but because if they don't then the real trouble will begin. Planets will flame into atomic destruction and millions will die. Die on both sides. Die beneath the insane logic of retribution, the 'hurt me and I'll hurt you double' code. And so space ships fire on each other. The fleets sometimes tangle in brief conflict, and life is made almost impossible for the small trader.'

His voice died into silence, ebbing in faint echoes against the metal of the hull and bulkheads, and he swayed a little, his magnetic boots holding his feet to the deck-plates and giving a semblance of gravity. Warren glowered and stamped over to the gutted ruin of the generator.

'Why aren't you working?' he snapped at the big engineer. 'I understood that this ship carried competent personnel, yet all I've seen you do is sit there and look at that machine.'

'That's right,' said Handley calmly.

'Well? Why don't you fix it then?'

'Why should I?' Handley rose slowly to his feet, his great bulk dwarfing the old man. 'If you're so worried about it, do it yourself.'

'That's impossible. I'm a financier, not an engineer. I wouldn't know the first thing about it.'

'Then hadn't you better keep your mouth shut?' Handley didn't raise his voice, but something in his eyes made the old man glance hastily at the young commander.

'Ranson. Do you permit your underlings to address your employer that way?'

'What?' Ranson jerked himself awake and stared at the two men. 'What's the trouble?'

'This engineer of yours refuses to repair the ship. When I spoke to him about it, he insulted me.' Warren's voice echoed with a brittle menace in the silence of the ship. 'I warn you, Ranson. I've broken men for saying less, and I could break you, too. I know how you Free Traders operate. Always in debt, always praying for a stroke of luck, half of

11

you begging your fuel and the rest running close to the edge of the law. I was a fool to have chartered you, but while I'm on board this ship I'll have respect.'

'Will you?' Ranson didn't sound worried. He swayed and yawned, his grey eyes dull with fatigue. 'How much sleep have you had since we were attacked Warren?'

'I don't know, the usual amount, I suppose. Why?'

'Handley and I haven't slept at all in the ten days we've been drifting here. We've kept going on drugs, doing without sleep, trying to get this wreck into some sort of repair. Believe me, Warren, we are just as anxious to stay alive as you are. We have done our best, but our best wasn't good enough, we can't repair the ship. As he told you earlier, this is the end of the line. We've had it, Warren, all of us. Do you understand what I mean?'

'You're joking, trying to frighten me, trying to make a fool of an old, helpless man.' Warren stared at the young commander, his greying features sickly in the guttering light of the candles.

'I thought that you hadn't grasped it.' Ranson shook himself a little and his eyes cleared as he saw the fear in Warren's pale eyes. 'We are helpless, devoid of energy without power to operate the air purifiers, radio, the lights, anything depending on electrical current. We've lived on tanked air and worked by candlelight. The food in the deep freeze is rotten and the thermocans are nearly finished.' He stared at the dancing flame of the candles. 'When the air goes — then so do we.'

'Then blow them out! They use oxygen, don't they?'

'Yes, they use oxygen, not much, but they do use it.' He stared at Warren. 'Would you like me to blow them out? If I do we can all sit in the dark — waiting. Is that what you want?'

'No. I — ' Sweat glistened on the wrinkled skin. 'Damn it, Ranson, you can't let me die like this! I'm a rich man! I'll give you anything, anything at all if you'll get me back to Earth alive. Please, Ranson, the joke has gone on for long enough! Tell me what you want and let's get on our way.'

'What are you talking about?' The young commander frowned as he looked at the old man. Warren gulped and his pale eyes glittered as he glanced from one to the other of the two men.

'I've heard tales of you Free Traders,' he whispered. 'They warned me not to charter you, but I was in a hurry and it was essential that I go to Deneb IV. You've fixed this haven't you? You want me to give you more money. I know how it is, this wouldn't be the first time a Free Trader has held his passenger to ransom. Well, damn you, you've won! How much?'

'Twenty million,' said Ranson calmly, then, as he saw the expression on the old man's features, anger rose within him. 'Why, you senile old fool! Do you think that I've killed six of my men, wrecked my ship, and risked my life for your lousy money? Damn you, Warren. I've a mind to throw you out of the airlock for what you've just said; I've heard of these tales you mention. I've heard them all over space, but I've yet to find anyone with any proof as to the truth of any one of them.

I'm not saying that all the Free Traders are angels, they're not, but how far do you think they would get if they did as you say? I'll tell you. It would happen once, no more, and then they'd be blasted from space by every honest Trader within the Rim.'

'Then — ' Fear broke the skin of the old man into a million tiny wrinkles, and his pale eyes widened with a horrible certainty. 'You aren't scaring me? You really do mean that we are all going to die?'

'Yes.'

'No!' Warren crouched against the bulkhead, his mouth open and his thin figure trembling with naked fear. 'It can't be! It can't! Not to me! Not to me!'

'To all of us.' Ranson shrugged and turned away from the naked emotion mirrored on the old man's face. He could understand how Warren felt, but, even though he understood it, he still didn't like to see it. Warren was like all of those on the safe planets. He was like any one of a million rich men who had been used to controlling their destinies by means of their wealth. Unpleasant things could happen — but not to them. Others could die and suffer in the lonely wastes of space, but not them. They sat in their offices and controlled the passenger transports, the trading vessels, the whole of the interstellar commerce by means of their cartels and monopolies. Only the Free Traders and a few independents remained outside the ring of the financial empire, the rest worked for the few.

Warren was one of the few. A genius in his own field he had gained control of one of the basic industries and every ship that lifted itself into space paid tribute to his fuel empire. He had never known personal danger. He had never yet met a situation out of which he could not buy his way. Now, when the harsh truth of reality stared him in the face, he could not bring himself to accept the inevitable. He could not believe that his one sure weapon, the one thing which had always served him in the past, could help him no longer.

He couldn't accept the fact that he was unable to buy his life.

Almost Ranson felt sorry for him.

Mechanically he moved across the cluttered engine room to the rank of oxygen bottles, his long fingers twisting their valves. As he had known they were open, the gas compressed within the tanks exhausted and he shrugged as he sniffed at the stale air.

'We could get into the suits,' said Handley quietly. The engineer leaned against a stanchion, breathing in shallow gasps, rationing himself to the basic minimum of the precious gas. Ranson nodded.

'Agreed, but what then? The vortex gun would have drained the batteries, so we'd have no heat, no radio communication, nothing we haven't got here. Personally, I'd rather die here, where I've got room to move about, than lock myself in the coffin of a space suit.'

'The tanks would keep us alive.'

'Why? What do you expect to happen? A rescue party?'

'Maybe, some funny things can happen in space. For all we know there's a ship headed straight towards us. Those extra few hours of life could make all the difference.'

'Perhaps.' Ranson shrugged, not giving the matter a second thought. He knew that the engineer was talking more for the benefit of the old man than for any other reason. He knew that the chances of a rescue ship intercepting their flight path was so remote as to be almost non-existent, but men, when they are facing death, do peculiar things.

Abruptly Ranson stretched out his hand towards the candles.

'You could be right,' he said, and pinched out one of the tiny flames. 'We'll take a chance that you are. The suits can wait until the air gets a lot worse than it is, and the smell won't kill us.' A second candle died between his thumb and forefinger. 'I'll kill the lights and we'll try to get some rest. Use less oxygen that way.' Again he reached for the guttering flame of the candles and shadows crept forward from where they lurked in the angle of the bulkheads.

'Wait!' Warren nervously licked his lips as he stared at the remaining candle.

'Can't we leave just one alight? I'm not tired and the darkness will send me crazy.'

'It uses oxygen,' said Ranson, but his hand fell away from the tiny flame. 'Very well, then, we'll leave it alight. Stay awake, Warren, and call me if anything happens.' He grinned at the old man and settled himself in a comfortable attitude, his heavy lids drooping over his sore eyes.

His last impression was that of a wrinkled, scared, almost yellow face hovering, as though disembodied, in the tiny light of an archaic candle. Then darkness closed in around him, muffling his overstrained, overtired senses, and he slept.

2

The Ginzoes

He awoke to naked fear.

Something battered against him, something hard and painful, bruising his flesh and shocking his nerves with the force of its impact. Dimly, as if from a vast distance, he heard the sounds of ragged breathing and a low whisper of desperate words.

'Ranson! Wake up, damn you! Wake up, man! Wake up!'

He rolled, grabbing at whatever it was that struck against him, opening his eyes and wincing as the soft yellow light stabbed into his brain. Something soft twisted in his grip and a man whimpered with pain. Abruptly he awoke, shaking his head to clear it from the foggy mists of sleep, and stared down at the fear-twisted features of the old man.

'Warren!' He pushed the financier

away. 'Were you hitting me?'

'Yes. You wouldn't wake up. I called and called and still you slept. I had to hit you.'

'Well?' Ranson rested his temples against his palms. 'What's all the excitement about?'

'There's something outside the ship.' Warren gulped and wiped sweat from his wrinkled features. 'I first heard it about ten minutes ago, and I've been trying to wake you ever since.'

'A noise?' Ranson cocked his head and gestured for silence. 'Are you certain? I can't hear anything.'

'It stopped just before you awoke.'

'Did it?' The young commander stared at the old man. He felt sluggish and his stomach burned from lack of rest and proper food. The drugs he had taken in order to remain awake now demanded their penalty and he knew that nothing but a long, deep sleep would restore his normal quickness and mental clarity. 'Silence and imagination can play peculiar tricks, Warren. Are you certain that you heard an external sound?'

'I heard it,' said the old man stubbornly. 'A bump and a grating sound. Then it stopped for a while and started again. What could it be, Ranson?'

'How do I know?' Ranson surged to his feet as the implications of what the old man said registered on his sleep-dulled senses. 'Unless it is in line with the direct vision ports there's no way of telling. The visi-screen went out with the rest of the electrical gear when the vortex gun sucked our energy.' He frowned down at the sleeping engineer. 'Wake Handley. You don't have to beat him to death as you tried to do to me, just put your hand over his mouth and nose, he'll wake when he finds that he can't breath.'

'Is it a rescue ship?' Warren stared up from where he crouched over the sleeping engineer. Ranson shrugged.

'It could be, or — ' He stiffened as sound penetrated from the hull. A peculiar grinding, shrilling sound as of a diamond pointed drill or a circular saw. 'I'm going to the control room to see whether or not I can spot what is making that noise. You stay here — and wake

Handley.' His metal-soled boots clattered on the deck plates as he almost ran towards the control room.

Like the rest of the ship the instrument-littered control room was in total darkness, but here, covered now by the solar screens, were the direct vision ports, small round windows of toughened plastic and normally used only for emergency astrogation. Carefully the young commander slid aside one of the screens and peered at the star-shot night of outer space.

Nothing!

Again his nerves jumped as sound rasped through the hull and quivered the stale air with the force of its vibrations. Another screen slid aside, another, and he stooped, his eyes narrowed as he stared at what was limned against the glittering backdrop of space.

When he finally straightened, his eyes were bleak, and his lips had thinned to a fine, almost cruel line against the hard contours of his face. Slowly he returned to the engine room and Handley stared up at him from where he sat, blinking and rubbing the base of his neck.

'Well?' The engineer winced as the jarring sound drummed from the outer hull.

'The old man was right,' said Ranson quietly. 'We seem to have been discovered.'

'I knew it!' Warren almost sobbed with relief. 'It's a rescue party, isn't it? I knew that I wasn't going to die out here. It couldn't happen to me. It couldn't!'

'Is he right?' Handley rose slowly to his feet. 'Is it a rescue party?'

'I'm not sure.' Ranson stared at the point from which the sound appeared to be coming. 'It's a ship right enough, but whether or not it's a rescue party is another matter.'

'How so?'

'It's an enemy ship. A Ginzo vessel!' Ranson stared at their shocked expressions. 'They probably saw us drifting and have come after us. We know that they've captured Terran vessels before, they are probably interested in how the hyperdrive works, and they must want this ship for the same reason.'

'Shouldn't we destroy it, then?'

'And us with it?' Ranson shook his

24

head as the big engineer hesitated. 'It isn't necessary, Handley. Their vortex guns have done an excellent job of ruining everything workable. Not even a Terran workshop with a full knowledge of the hyper-drive could repair it, and the Ginzoes haven't a chance of discovering anything with their totally different technology.' He stared at the quivering hull. 'We have had the same trouble with ships which have fallen into our hands. Aside from the fact that they don't use the hyper-drive we don't know a thing about them. Even their basic chemistry is different from ours.'

'Then why do they want the ship?'

'Why do we want theirs? Hope, I guess. The faint hope that an undamaged vessel can teach them something they don't already know.'

'I see.' Handley licked his lips and dabbed at his glistening features. 'What are we going to do, Carl? If they find us here they will kill us.'

'Perhaps.'

'How do you mean 'perhaps'?' The engineer glowered at the young commander. 'We're at war, aren't we? They blasted us, didn't they? Well? Why shouldn't they kill us?'

'Why should they? We haven't shot Ginzoes when we've had the chance to take them prisoner. They are an intelligent race and maybe they will act in an intelligent fashion.' Ranson sniffed at the foetid air. 'In any case, we've got to chance it. Unless we get out of it we'll be dead within another day.'

He turned, and opening a locker, removed several space suits. The shapeless objects with their tanks of air drifted in the gravity-free engine room and the big engineer grabbed at them, inspecting them with expert eyes. 'These aren't much good without the electronic equipment, Carl.'

'They'll serve their purpose. We'll wear them, seal them and wait for the Ginzoes to find us.'

'You think that it will work?'

'I don't know, but what can we lose? Hurry now! Get into your suit!'

Hastily the engineer climbed into the tough fabric and metal of the space suit. Ranson followed his example and together the two men helped the old man to don the protective clothing. Carefully they strapped and adjusted the suit around the thin figure, then, his faceplate open, Ranson gave swift instructions.

'Now, the way the Ginzoes operate is the same as we do when we find a wrecked vessel. They will drill the hull or wrench open the airlock. Evacuate the ship and blow out the air. Then they will either send a party aboard in suits or they will connect both ships with a communication tube and fill the ship with their own air. In either case, we must be protected with spacesuits. Now. Close your faceplates and turn on the air tanks. Let the pressure rise until your ears ring, swallowing will ease the pressure after a time. Make no move. That is important. Make no move at all.'

Carefully he stretched his gloved hand towards the solitary candle, then paused as the tiny flame danced and quivered. Around them rose a thin whining, a high-pitched hissing and he grunted as he felt the stale air move against his sweating features.

'They've penetrated the hull! Close your helmets. Hurry!'

Swiftly he closed his own helmet and turned on the air tanks. He swallowed as the rising pressure caused his ears to ring, then, steadily, he snuffed out the candle.

Darkness closed around them as they waited in the silence of the airless ship.

For a long time nothing happened and Ranson sweated inside the confines of his space suit. He sweated, but he knew that unless circumstances altered soon he would freeze as his body heat radiated away, not replaced by the drained energy cells. Sounds came to him, transmitted through the metal of the deck plates and carried to his ears by his metal-soled boots and bone conduction. Sharp sounds, made by the impact of metal on metal, and together with the sounds came the scintillating fury of an electronic torch as it sliced its way through the stubborn metal of the inner hull.

Abruptly a section of the hull fell away and stars gleamed in the gap. Stars, and something else!

The Ginzoes were not humanoid. They

did not have two arms, two legs, a head and a similar metabolism to that of the human race. In shape, in mental processes, in their technology and chemistry, they were alien, and the shape that stood, limned in the brilliant glitter of the cold stars was like something from a drug-induced nightmare.

It was squat, many legged, tentacled, and spined. It was repulsive, strange, insect-like and nonhuman, and yet Ranson knew that within the distorted shape reposed a keen intelligence and active brain. He stiffened, his eyes narrowed as he watched the alien cautiously enter the ship and light flickered from one of the thing's many appendages, It gleamed from the ruined machines, reflecting from the blank surfaces of the dead glo-plates and the plastic tubes of the dark fluorescents. It danced in a clean circle over the interior of the engine room, passed over one of the space suited figures, hesitated, swung — and Ranson blinked in a sudden glare.

For a moment he remained motionless, knowing that the alien could see his features through the transparent plastic of his faceplate, then, moving with an exaggerated slowness, he carefully lifted his right arm.

The alien jerked, a scuttling backwards motion, and metal gleamed at the tip of one tentacle, as it raised a weapon. Ranson swallowed, tensing his stomach muscles against abrupt destruction, and gritted his teeth as he forced his arm to continue its upward gesture.

Nothing happened.

No blasting shaft of energy, no tearing missile or lambent ray spat from the mysterious weapon, and Ranson breathed easier as he realised that his gesture had been understood. Cautiously he stepped forward, raising his other arm, and stood before the alien both arms lifted, both hands turned, palms forward, towards the alien in the universal gesture of peace.

Slowly both Handley and Warren repeated his movements and the three of them stood side by side — waiting.

Finally the Ginzo moved. It moved with a flurry of tentacles, jerking sideways with fantastic speed, and behind it, in the gap sliced in the hull, other nightmares pressed forward, their tentacle-lights illuminating the entire interior of the engine room. They scuttled around the three motionless figures, disappearing into the other regions of the vessel, and their lights cast grotesque shadows on the bulkheads and hull. Again came a period of silent watching, and Ranson slowly lowered his arms, biting his lips against the ache in his muscles, and yet, despite his pain, interested in what he saw.

The Ginzo was not human and did not have the stiff rigidity of a human form. Its protective covering was supple and transparent and Ranson stared at the form within the flexible envelope. It was big, half as big again as a man, and its thick, barrel-like body sprouted append-ages at either end. The lower ones served as legs while the upper, thinner and more flexible, served as arms and other organs. Some of the tentacles carried eyes, others mouths, some had strong, pincer-like claws, while others had delicate filaments capable of fine work and suited for intricate manoeuvring. Deep within the thick body reposed the brain, shielded and safe from harm, and both body and appendages were protected by a tough though flexible outer skin.

This Ranson knew, and knowing that, knew almost all there was to be known of the Ginzoes. The rest was based on sheer speculation. It was assumed that they communicated by a medium similar to radio waves. How they reproduced was a mystery. It was known that they lived a communal life similar to ants or bees, and while a Ginzo could, with the proper instruments, communicate with a man, yet a man could not even begin to talk to a Ginzo. All communication between the two races was conducted in Terran, and it was a source of constant irritation to the semantic experts that it had been the aliens who had devised the sole method of communication known.

Now, man and alien stood and stared at each other in the steady glare of tentacle-lights within the confines of a wrecked vessel.

Ranson bit his lips at a sudden movement at his side. He half-turned, his

32

arms moving in an instinctive gesture, then froze, his nerves quivering, as the alien scuttled forward. Between them a space suited figure slumped silently to the deck plates.

Warren? Handley? Ranson cursed the lack of radio communication, then, as he stared at the thin figure, knew that it must have been the old man who had fainted. Both he and the big engineer were spacemen enough to have grown used to alien life forms, but the old financier, sheltered on the safe planets, had never known the many shapes which intelligence could take. Now he had seen one of the mysterious enemy at close range, and the sight had proved too much for him. Ranson shrugged, half-contemptuous, half-disgustedly, then turned again and faced the alien. Ugly or not, enemy or not, the Ginzoes were their only hope. Ranson could only hope that curiosity or some other reason would drive them to rescue the three men.

But he had little hope that they would.

The searchers returned to the engine room. They scuttled around in ordered confusion, seeming to study the snarled mass of the generator and standing in a compact group around the squat bulk of the hyper-drive unit. They stared at it for a long time, then, as if acting on a common impulse, they fetched tools, and fire scintillated from strange devices as they cut the massive unit from its base. They lifted it, carrying it carefully through the gap in the hull, and Ranson knew that they had done that for which they came.

Finally they turned their attention to the three men.

Tentacles reached out, caught hold of the slumped figure on the deck plates, lifted it, carried it towards the sliced hull. Others reached for Ranson and the engineer, and the young commander relaxed as he felt himself being lifted. They were safe!

They had aroused the curiosity of the aliens, and the Ginzoes, for reasons of their own, had decided to rescue the three Terrans. Perhaps for questioning, for testing, for vivisection, or to be exhibited in a zoo. Ranson didn't know and at the moment he didn't care.

He slumped, yielding to the demands of his outraged body, then, as the shock of reaction, the ten-day sleepless period, the after effects of too many drugs and lack of proper food and air gripped him, sank into a semi-coma.

Dimly he was aware of the short journey between the two ships, the green-yellow atmosphere within the alien vessel and nightmare shapes bending over him, their stalk-eyes glaring into his face plate. Then everything seemed to recede into a yellow mist shot with weaving tentacles and green streaks of stabbing light.

He never knew when he reached the end of his journey.

3

Ultimatum

The air was heavy with the reek of chlorine, but it was breathable and didn't have the taint of seared flesh and rotting waste. Ranson breathed it, cautiously inhaling it through his nostrils, feeling the chlorine grip his lungs and then coughing to expel the poison.

'Watch your breathing,' he warned. 'Take small, shallow breaths, the chlorine in here isn't too healthy.'

'I know that.' Handley nodded from where he rested on a narrow bunk. 'It's getting better, though.' He glanced to where the old man lay in uneasy slumber on the second of three bunks. 'How's the old man?'

'He'll live.' Ranson swung his legs over the edge of his bunk and frowned at the bare metal walls of the room. 'What happened after they grabbed us? I must have passed out or something. I remember them lifting us, carrying us into their ship, then everything went hazy and the lights went out. Did you stay conscious?'

'Just about.' The engineer stared at the low ceiling. 'They must have built this place just for us. They sealed it, sucked out the chlorine, and piped in some sort of apology for air. I kept my suit on until it was fit to breathe, then stripped and removed both of your suits. The air in the tanks made it easier to breathe in here. Then I dropped off and when I awoke things were just as you see them.'

'No suits?' Ranson stared about the tiny room.

'They must have removed them after you fell asleep.' He shrugged. 'Not that it matters. We have breathable air, are riding in a ship that is going somewhere other than drifting to Hell, and so far they seem to have taken care of us.'

'Yes,' said Handley slowly. 'That is what's worrying me.'

'What is? The fact that you are still alive?'

'No. The thought of what they may be

keeping me alive for.'

'I know what you mean.' Ranson stared grimly at the walls of the bare room. 'I don't like it any more than you do, but what choice had we?'

'None, but I'd have felt a lot happier going out with a flare-gun in each hand and taking a few of them with me.'

'Now you're going too fast and too far. We have no proof that they intend us any harm.'

'We're at war, aren't we?' Handley twisted on the narrow bunk and stared at the young commander. 'They blasted us, didn't they? Well? What's to stop them playing some fancy tricks on us?'

'Nothing, but why should they?'

'Can't you answer that one, or are you just making noises with your mouth?' The engineer wiped sweat from his broad features. 'You know as well as I do what happens to Ginzoes unlucky enough to be captured alive. Some of them are split open to find out what makes them tick. Others are teased a little to make them talk, a few are kept as controls and some help to make our zoos the interesting places they are.' He spat, his disgust evident in every gesture. 'Those dumb swine back on the safe planets think they can win this war the easy way. I know that they can't, you know it, every man who has ever been to space knows it. Damn it to hell! Why can't they declare a peace and live and let live?'

'They've been at it for ten years now,' said Ranson quietly. 'You think that they're going to stop now?'

'Why not?'

'If we stop, will they? Will the Ginzoes quit fighting if we do? And if they will, how are we going to arrange the peace? No, Handley, I agree with you in that this war should never have started, but I'm remembering Altair and the twenty million dead. This war is a bad thing, but it could be a lot worse. Rather have what we've got than chance a real, knock-down-drag-'em-out conflict which can only hurt innocent people and ruin interstellar trade!'

'Yeah.' Handley grunted as he relaxed on his bunk. 'Maybe you're right. I wouldn't know. I'm just a dumb engineer with his brains all in his two hands. Space travel isn't hard enough, what with the danger of air-leak, energy failure, ultra-sonic and mistimed emergence. We have to have ships waiting for us with loaded guns. And why? Because some brass hat thinks that we shouldn't have nasty aliens too near to our nice, money-spinning little planets. They make me sick!' He spat, his broad features twisted with disgust.

'I know,' said Ranson quietly. 'You don't have to tell me.'

'Don't I?' Handley twisted in his bunk and stared at the young commander. 'What's the matter with you, Carl? I've travelled with you for a long time now. I've seen you slave to earn money to buy your own ship, and then sweat blood to keep it in space. You're a Free Trader, man! What is this war to you? Why the hell didn't you head for the Rim, when I asked you to? If you had we'd have been out of this mess, with our own ship and a tidy pile in the bank. But you couldn't do that. Not you. You had to head towards the Centre, back to Earth, the home planet. You wanted to sell the ship and enlist in the space navy. I stopped you from selling the ship and you know what happened when you tried to enlist.'

'I know,' said Ranson bitterly. 'They turned me down. Fifteen years space experience, ten of them as pilot wasn't good enough for them. They only had room for graduates from the Space Academy, they didn't want me or anyone like me.' He sighed, his grey eyes dull as if at the pain of old hurts. 'I travelled more than a hundred light years to reach Earth. I thought that they wanted every man they could get, but I was wrong, I hadn't known about the unwritten agreement with the Ginzoes, and there is only room in the navy for the select few. Don't rub it in, Handley.'

'I'm not, but it's time that you learned sense. Why did you accept Warren's charter? You knew that he wanted to enter a C area. He wouldn't have hired you if he could have got there some other way. You risked everything you owned, everything you had worked and sweated for, and now it's all gone. Why did you do it, Carl?'

'Why?' Ranson shrugged and stared towards the sleeping man. 'Warren is rich,' he said slowly. 'He is worth more money than I ever hope to own, than any ten Free Traders are likely to own. Why should he be willing to risk his neck trying to enter a C area?'

'Money,' said the engineer promptly. 'Some people just can't get enough.'

'Perhaps, but Warren is rich, it would take a great deal of money to tempt such a man into personal danger.'

'Maybe he isn't as rich as everyone thinks. A lot of these financiers operate mostly on bluff. Perhaps he needs a lot of money quick to swing a deal or something. For all we know he might be on the very edge of bankruptcy.'

'You could be right,' said Ranson slowly, 'but somehow I don't think that you are. Warren is an old man, and old men tend to be careful of their skins. He knew the danger, despite what he said about the Free Traders having an agreement with the Ginzoes. Warren is no fool, no one with his amount of money could be, and he knew the risk. I'd like to know just why he wanted to go to Deneb IV.'

'Then why don't you ask him?' Handley pointed towards the old man. 'He's awake now. Get in quick before he gains full control of his senses. Sometimes you can shock the truth out of a man if you ask the right questions at the right time.'

Ranson nodded and slipped from his bunk.

Warren lay on his back, his wrinkled features yellow in the bright lighting and his breathing whistled through his flesh-less lips as his lungs fought the traces of chlorine tainting the air. He didn't move his head when the young commander stooped over him. He just stared with his pale blue eyes at the low ceiling and Ranson knew that the old man still hovered on the edges of sleep.

'Warren,' he said gently. 'Why did you want to go to Deneb IV?'

'Money.' The thin lips moved in a parody of a smile.

'But how, Warren? How did you hope to make money entering a C area?'

'What?' The old man blinked and nervously licked his thin lips. 'What are you talking about? Why are you questioning me?'

'I want to know why you hired me to take you to Deneb IV,' said Ranson tightly. Warren raised his sparse eyebrows.

'Isn't that obvious? I wanted to get there. Did you expect me to walk?'

'I want the truth, Warren! What took you to a planet deep in a C area? What is so valuable on Deneb IV that you risked your neck to get it?'

'That,' said Warren coldly, 'is my business. I intend that it shall remain my business.'

'Perhaps it's my business, too.' Ranson glared at the old man. 'We are in this together, Warren. I've lost my ship, six men of my crew and all I possess. I'd like to know just why I lost them.'

'Carelessness.' Warren shrugged and deliberately turned away from the young commander. 'Be your age, Ranson. I hired you to do a job. You failed. My personal affairs have nothing to do with either that failure or my charter. You have no right to question me. And you know it.'

Ranson rose from beside the bunk, knowing that the old man was right, and half-angry at himself for asking, and with Handley for prompting the question. Irritably he moved about the tiny room, studying the hasty welds and the obviously improvised inlet and outlet pipes for the air. The light came from a sheet of fluorescent material set flush into the ceiling and he stared at it, wondering whether or not it operated on the same principle as the glo-plates on Terran space ships. He shrugged, better minds than his had attempted to solve the secrets of an alien science and had failed. He could hardly hope to do what they had been unable to do with full equipment and unlimited time.

A grating sound came from one side of the room, and he tensed, fighting the instinctive hardening of his muscles, his eyes narrowed as he stared towards the source of the sound.

A panel slid to one side and a Ginzo entered the room.

It wore protective clothing, not a space suit but a lighter, more flexible garment, and within the transparency chlorine swirled in a green-yellow cloud. A second alien pushed a low trolley into the room, a trolley laden with instruments and with power cables snaking away towards the rear. A gush of chlorine entered with them, and Ranson felt his lungs tightening as he inhaled the poison, and he coughed, his breath strangling in his throat as he fought the yellow gas.

'By Hades, they want to communicate with us!' Handley gasped in the polluted air, his broad features glistening with perspiration, and stared curiously at the strange instruments. 'Either that or they are going to slice us open.'

'No.' Warren crouched against the metal wall, his wrinkled features distorted with fear. 'No. Don't let them touch me. Save me, Ranson. I'll give you anything you want, but save me!'

'Don't be a fool,' snapped Ranson. 'What could I do to save your skin? Anyway, I doubt if they intend us harm. Handley is right, they probably want to communicate with us.' He stared interestedly towards the two aliens and the instrument-loaded trolley.

A tentacle flipped a switch, power droned for a moment then died into whispering silence. A lamp glowed on a panel, needles flickered, and a fine-tipped appendage made a careful adjustment.

Abruptly words droned from the machine.

'Who is your speaker?'

'I am,' Ranson stepped forward and faced the two aliens and the strange machine. He knew that the Ginzoes did not have the same social structure as the Terrans, the idea of rank was alien to them. They operated as a complete unit with various members of that unit having specialised tasks. The term 'speaker' therefore meant literally what it said — 'one-who-speaks-for-all' — and he translated it into the Terran equivalent of Leader.

'Are you the directing head of your group?'

'Yes.'

'Director and Speaker?' Almost the droning words from the translation device echoed something of the alien's doubt. Ranson nodded and spoke directly at the suited alien.

'Our social structure is not as yours. Each of us is an individual, united for a common purpose but free to break from the group and operate alone or with others. I am the directing head of this group, the 'Leader' and I am also empowered to speak for all.'

'We understand.' The machine clicked and fell silent. Ranson guessed that the operator was busy communicating with the other aliens what he had just heard.

For a moment he wondered at a culture in which the first person singular did not exist, a culture in which the word 'I' did not have any place at all. No Ginzo, even when solitary and away from its own kind ever spoke in other than the plural 'we'. To their group culture the idea of personal individuality just did not exist. It had proved one of the biggest stumbling blocks in communication between the two races, and had created endless speculation among the semanticists.

Again the machine droned into life.

'What were you doing in this sector of space?'

'Heading for Deneb IV.'

'You knew the penalty for entering our area?'

'Yes.'

'Why did you want to land on Deneb IV?'

'I didn't, he did.' Ranson jerked his thumb towards Warren. 'I am a Free Trader, operating my own space ship, and the old man merely chartered me to give him transportation. Your vortex guns caught us as we emerged from hyperspace and set us adrift. You know the rest.'

'Hyperspace?'

'Our system of faster-than-light travel.' Ranson didn't offer to elaborate on his brief statement. Both sides were eager to learn the other's technique of faster-than-light travel, so far without success.

'Are you knowledgeable in the operation of your machines?'

'Yes.'

'Are you able to repair them?'

'Normally, yes, but if you hope that we can repair the hyper-drive unit you took

49

from my ship, you are wasting your time. Your vortex guns ruined it beyond repair.'

'We understand.' Again the machine clicked and fell silent as the alien communicated with its fellows. Ranson shifted uneasily on his feet. At the moment he had no personal fear, but he knew that a decision would have to be made and he wondered what it would be. Ginzoes captured by the Terrans were never set free. They were questioned, exhibited, tested, watched, and even, in the early days of the war, vivisected. He hoped that the enemy had gathered sufficient information about the human body structure to make further vivisection unnecessary.

The machine droned abruptly into life and emotionless words.

'We have considered. To keep you is not easy. Your kind require special food, water, air, and the benefits of keeping you are small.'

'They're going to kill us,' choked Handley, and Warren whimpered as he pressed his thin figure against the metal wall.

'Hold it,' snapped Ranson. 'They haven't said it yet. Let me handle this.' He turned to the machine with its enigmatic operator.

'Well?'

'We do not wish to destroy you. Such needless destruction is contrary to the Great Design, but we cannot expend energy to keep you without benefit to ourselves. We are faced with a problem.'

'That's what you think!' Handley snorted as he stared at the aliens. 'What about us?'

'Will you keep that big mouth shut!' Ranson glared at the engineer. 'They aren't used to dealing with more than one at a time. If you interrupt you may throw everything to hell. Let me handle it.'

He faced the machine.

'Could you not return our space suits and set us down on an oxygen world?'

'We would be destroyed.'

'Then set us adrift in space with a signal flare or radio.'

'We would be destroyed.'

'I see. Then is it your intention to kill us?'

'Yes, unless — '

'Unless, what?' Ranson swallowed, wishing that he faced a man instead of a machine. It was impossible to tell from the mechanical drone whether the operator was joking, teasing them, being sadistic, or meant exactly what he said.

'We do not wish to destroy intelligent life if it can be avoided. The Great Design forbids it, but we are a logical people and so must be ruled by logic. To keep you necessitates trouble, inconvenience, and an expenditure of energy. We have met this problem before. We have solved it, both for those of our own race and those of other intelligent races, and you are from an intelligent race. You, then, must solve your own problem.'

'How?' Ranson stared at the alien with mounting hope.

'Give us one good reason why you should not be destroyed.'

'What?'

'Cannot you understand? Unless you can give us one good reason for remaining alive we shall eliminate you. Your future depends on yourselves.'

'I understand,' said Ranson sickly. 'Have we time for thought?'

'Is it necessary?' Almost it seemed as if the alien shrugged. 'We shall go now and when we return you will tell us your reason — or be destroyed!'

Slowly both machine and aliens left the room.

4

Black bargain

It was simple. It was so simple that in a way it was ludicrous. To live, all they had to do was to give one good reason why they should not die. That was all, and thinking about it, Ranson felt his mouth dry and his stomach churn at the subtle intelligence behind the simple-seeming question.

The answer had to do more than satisfy themselves. It had to satisfy the Ginzoes, and a race that operated on a basis of cold logic would not be easily satisfied. They had to give the aliens one good reason why they should not be destroyed, one reason why the aliens should go to the trouble and expense of keeping them alive and well.

He stared at the taut faces of the others.

'Well?' He slumped down on to the

edge of his bunk. 'Any suggestions?'

Handley licked his lips with a quick, nervous gesture. 'You think that they mean what they say?'

'Yes.'

'They really intend killing us if we can't satisfy them?'

'Yes.'

'They can't do that!' Warren surged to his feet, his wrinkled features twisted with fear. 'They can't kill us just as if we were vermin! We are men! Terrans! They can't kill us!'

'Are you trying to convince them or yourself?' Ranson thinned his lips in a tight, humourless smile. 'They can do anything they wish to us, and we can't stop them. Get rid of the idea that they can't do it. They can. And they will unless we play the game their way.'

'Well then, we'll play it their way.' Handley shrugged and relaxed on his bunk. 'The answer's easy enough. I don't want them to kill me because I want to stay alive. Simple.'

'Is it?' Ranson shook his head.

'Start thinking like that and we'll all

die. You miss the point, Handley. The Ginzoes aren't interested in our reasons to ourselves, they are only interested in our reasons to them. The mere fact that you don't want to die is meaningless. No one wants to die, but is that any reason for keeping them alive?'

'It is to them,' grunted the engineer, 'but I see what you mean.'

'We've got to convince the Ginzoes that we will be worth our keep,' explained Ranson tightly. 'And we had better start thinking along strictly logical lines. Once we let emotion dull our judgment — we're sunk. The Ginzoes aren't emotional.'

Ranson stared at the intent faces of the others.

'Any suggestions?'

'I don't want to die,' said Handley slowly, then shook his head. 'No. You mustn't kill me because — ' He grinned at the young commander. 'Now I see what you mean. We've got to bargain for our lives.' His heavy features contorted with thought. 'Now what can we offer the Ginzoes to make it worth their while to keep us?'

'Money.' Warren thrust himself forward, his pale blue eyes glittering. 'Offer them money, as much of it as they want. That should do the trick.'

'They don't use money,' said Ranson wearily. 'They have an economy based on units of energy. Try again.'

'Perhaps we can persuade them to keep us for exchange. Retain us to swap for Ginzoes caught by the Terran fleet?'

'Not good enough.' Ranson stared at the engineer. 'How about you, Handley?'

'It took forty years for me to learn what I know,' said the engineer slowly, and it seemed as if he spoke more to himself than to the other men. 'To kill me would be a waste of that knowledge.'

'Better, but not good enough. What does your knowledge mean to the Ginzoes? They couldn't use it. No, Handley, it's no use appealing to their sympathy or sentiment. They haven't got any.' He frowned down at the bare floor, trying to imagine what he would do, how he would feel if the positions were reversed.

It wasn't easy.

Death was such a personal thing. To the individual it was all-important but to others it was nothing. It mattered only to the person it affected, and to find one good reason why any single man should be permitted to live —

He thinned his lips as he thought about it. Aside from common humanity, sentiment, a quirk of emotion or bare charity, there wasn't one valid reason why any of Terra's billions should be allowed to live. Not a single person would affect the course of events if they were blotted out. A few scientists perhaps, a few research workers striving to solve a few of the secrets of nature, but even then they were not really important. To others, that is, and to an alien race who cared nothing for the progress of their enemies they would be better dead than alive.

For the first time Ranson began to appreciate the subtlety of an alien sense of humour.

For, of course, there was no answer. Nothing he could possibly say would convince the Ginzoes that he was indispensable. His private hopes, fears, ambitions, meant nothing to them. His longing for life, his unfinished business, his responsibilities and commitments, none of these would help to sway the balance in his favour. Even thinking about them was a waste of time.

And time was running out.

Grimly he stared at the bare floor and squeezed his temples between the thumb and forefinger of his right hand. One good reason. Just one! It would serve for all of them, for the Ginzoes, with their group culture, would accept it for the three. One good reason between the three of them for staying alive. Ranson sweated as he realised that only an egocentric of the worst degree could honestly claim that his death would be a loss to the world. What reason could he give strong enough and logical enough for the aliens to decide that they were worth keeping?

What reason could any man give?

On one of the other bunks Warren bared his yellow teeth in an animal-snarl, and Ranson stared at the old man with suspicious curiosity. The old financier wasn't acting in character. He should have been trembling with fear, almost paralysed with it, desperate for the others to find the answer. Instead of which he rested on his bunk, staring at the two men with his pale blue eyes, snarling as if impatient at their delay.

Almost as if he had the answer, but didn't want to use it.

Ranson stared at him, at the thin, withered hands and the wrinkled skin, then, acting on sudden impulse, surged from his bunk in smoothly coordinated motion. Warren gaped at him, twisted, then bared his teeth in silent anger as his thin hands clawed at the wrists of the young commander.

'Ranson! Have you gone insane?' Handley stepped forward. 'What are you throttling the old man for?'

'Keep out of this, Handley.' Ranson grinned down at the convulsed features of the financier. 'Well, Warren?' Slowly he tightened his hands around the scrawny throat. 'Give me one good reason why I shouldn't kill you!'

'Let me go, you fool!' Warren gulped and tugged at the young commander's wrists. 'Are you mad?'

'No, Warren, I'm not mad, but I think that you know the answer. If you don't, then I'm sorry for you, because, Warren, if you don't give it to me, I'm going to kill you!'

'Carl! You can't mean it!' Handley stared at the old man, then slowly stepped away from the two men.

'You do mean it,' he whispered. 'Warren. If you have the answer, tell him. Tell him, quick!'

'Leave me alone, you fool!' The old man surged, and Ranson was surprised at the strength hidden in the thin body. He surged, struggled for a moment, then relaxed on the bunk, sweat streaming from his wrinkled features.

'Let me go,' he babbled. 'Let me talk to them alone. I'll find a way out, I promise it.'

'Talk.' Deliberately Ranson tightened his grip. Knowing that the old man was suffering more from his own imagination than from any actual danger. Warren gulped.

'I'll give you money,' he whined. 'Lots of money. I'll work for you, do anything you want. I'll help you. I'll — '

'That's enough.' Ranson released his grip on the scrawny throat and stared thoughtfully down at the gasping old man. 'I'll help you,' he said slowly. 'I'll help — ' He turned away from the bunk and stared at the engineer. 'Handley! Did you hear that?'

'Hear what?'

'The answer! The thing that can save us! Didn't you hear it?'

'No.' Handley frowned, and his big body sagged. 'Do you feel all right, Carl? This air's pretty bad, and you've been through a lot. Why not lie down for a while?'

'Don't talk like a fool, Handley, I'm not insane. Warren has just given us the answer: Didn't you get what he said?'

'No.'

'He offered to help us,' explained the young commander. 'To work for us.'

'Well?' Handley stared blankly at the young man. 'What of it?'

'Damn you, Handley, must you be so dumb? Doesn't what he said give you an idea?' Ranson stared at the engineer.

'Reverse it! Suppose that we were to offer to help the Ginzoes? Wouldn't that be a reason for keeping us alive?'

'Perhaps,' agreed Handley slowly. 'But would they be satisfied with just an offer of help?'

'No, and that is where you come in.' Ranson sat down on the edge of a bunk. 'You said that you had spent forty years learning what you know. You have knowledge the Ginzoes could use, and will use if they can.'

'What knowledge?'

'It will be illogical to kill us,' said Ranson quietly, as if he were talking to the aliens rather than to the men in the room. 'If we are destroyed it will mean that you have lost your one chance of discovering how we can travel at faster-than-light speeds.'

'You mean — ' Handley stared in shocked amazement at the young commander.

'Yes. Our reason for not being destroyed is that we are willing to solve the secret of the hyper-drive for the Ginzoes.'

'No!' Savagely the engineer sprang to his feet.

'Damn it, Carl. I won't do it! Too many men have lost their lives protecting the secret for me to betray them now. No, Carl! You'll have to think of something else.'

'What?' Ranson stared coldly at the big man; 'You think of something, I can't. All I know is that they are interested in the hyper-drive. If we offer to repair a captured unit they may decide it is worthwhile to keep us alive and well.'

'No!'

'Get hold of yourself, Handley! I said we'd tell them that. What we really do is something else again.' He nodded as understanding dawned on the engineer's broad features. 'Yes. We lie to them, lie like heroes, and pray that they don't know it. One thing is in our favour, a logical race would never lie. It would be illogical to say one thing and mean another. We will promise to repair a hyper-drive unit — and they may think that a good reason for not destroying us.'

'Do you think that it will work?'

'I don't know,' said Ranson grimly. 'If it doesn't, none of us will leave this room alive. We'd better start hoping, and, if you happen to know a few prayers, they might help, too.'

Silently they settled down to wait for the return of the aliens.

They came as before, two of them, one pushing a small trolley on which rested the translating machine. They wasted no time.

'We have come for your answer.'

Ranson took a deep breath, glanced at the others, then faced the machine,

'It would be illogical to kill those who are in a position to benefit your race,' he said evenly, and wished that he could wipe the sweat from his streaming features.

'That is correct.' The drone from the machine startled him, he hadn't expected an answer to his rhetorical statement.

'We are in such a position.'

'Explain.'

'You have taken the hyper-drive unit from our ship. That particular unit was ruined by your vortex gun, but you may have others, some not so badly damaged. Is that the case?'

'Yes.'

'If you destroy us you will lose a chance of solving the method of their operation. We are willing to repair a hyper-drive unit and explain to you how it works. Therefore, destroying us would be illogical, and it would be to your benefit to keep us alive.'

For a long moment Ranson stared at the silent machine, hearing soft clicks coming from its interior, and knowing that the aliens were communicating with other of their kind. He felt a peculiar relief, a lessening of tension, a relaxing of his muscles and nerves. He had tried. If he had failed that couldn't be helped, but he had done his best and now there was nothing more he could do. Either the answer was one that would appeal to the aliens or it was not. If it were, they would live, if not, they would die.

It was as simple as that.

The machine clicked again and droned into life.

'You have the knowledge of repair?'

'We have.'

'Yet you say that you could not repair

the unit taken from your vessel?'

'No. Your weapon ruined it beyond repair. I make no wild promises, but, if you have an undamaged unit, we will repair, tune, operate and teach you the basic fundamentals of hyper-flight. We can do no more.'

Again there was silence as the aliens conferred, then —

'We accept. You will be kept. You will be taken to a place and there given tools and further instructions. That is all. You may rest now.'

The machine clicked. The aliens left. And all three men sighed in deep relief.

'We did it!' Handley grinned at the young commander. 'We fooled them!'

'Did we?' Ranson stared thoughtfully at the pipes thrusting into the room, the two pipes connected to the air system. 'Somehow I don't like it. There was no argument, no discussion, no questioning.'

'They believed us, didn't they?' Handley refused to be worried. 'We did it, I tell you! Everything's going to be all right.'

'You have doubts.' Warren stared at Ranson as he made the statement. 'Why?'

67

'Would we have acted like that if we had questioned a Ginzo?' Ranson bit his lips as he stared at the air pipe. 'I was a fool. I forgot to take the most elementary precautions, and I made the biggest mistake it is possible for a man to make. I've underestimated the enemy.'

'What do you mean, Carl?' Handley lost his grin as he saw the worried expression on the other's face. 'You think that they're playing with us?'

'I don't know, but I know what I would have done had I captured three Ginzoes. I'd have left them alone free to talk, thinking that they are safe from outside interference.' He tightened his fist and slammed it with brutal force against a wall. 'I'd forgotten all about one-way communication. Because we couldn't have learned anything from them I assumed that they couldn't, or wouldn't, listen to us.'

'Listen to us?' Handley swallowed as he realised what the young man was getting at. 'You think — '

'Why not? They came pretty soon after we'd reached a decision, didn't they?'

Ranson twisted his lips in a bitter expression of self-contempt. 'And I thought that we were being clever! Damn it! If those things can laugh, I bet they are rolling on the floor at this moment.'

'What are you talking about?' Warren nervously licked his thin lips. 'I don't understand.'

'Don't you?' Ranson strode towards the air pipe and wrenched it away from the wall. A puff of chlorine made him cough with sudden pain, and he stared into the revealed opening with watering eyes.

'That's what I'm talking about,' he said bitterly and stepped aside so that the others could see.

There, gleaming softly in the dim lighting, revealed by the removal of the air pipe, rested a small, grilled-fronted instrument. Handley swore and reached for it with one big hand.

'An ear! Damn it, Ranson, they had this room tapped all the time!'

'Leave it alone, Handley.' The young man knocked aside the reaching hand. Slowly he replaced the air pipe, stemming the leaking cloud of chlorine and slowly they returned to their bunks.

'They heard every word we said.' Handley dabbed at the sweat streaming from his broad face. 'They knew what we intended all the time.' He twisted and stared at the young commander. 'But if they knew what we intended, why didn't they kill us? What are they after?'

Ranson shrugged, not answering, still feeling sick at his own neglect at not searching for the microphone before making plans.

Now the aliens knew the exact measure of their sincerity. They knew that the last thing the Terrans intended was to reveal the operation of a hyper-drive unit. They knew all that, and yet they had done nothing about it.

Ranson wondered what it was all about.

5

The traitor

Time passed slowly in the small, bare metal room. They ate a tasteless grey paste and drank water reeking with the taint of chlorine. They slept, woke, slept again, and time became a meaningless period broken only by the infrequent meals.

'You know,' said Handley, grimacing over his grey paste, 'the Ginzoes must have gone to a lot of trouble over us. They've had to synthethise the air, the water, even the food. It couldn't have been easy at short notice.'

'I know.'

'I wondered whether we would have gone to all that trouble, Carl? It would have been so much easier to have killed us.'

'They didn't.' Ranson glanced to where the old man rested, asleep on his bunk.

'Handley! Have you noticed something funny about Warren?'

'Funny?'

'Yes, peculiar. He seems to sleep when we are awake. I half-woke a short time ago and saw him with his head close to the air pipe. It looked to me as if he were — whispering.'

'Talking to the Ginzoes?' The engineer looked startled. 'Are you sure, Carl? Why should he do that?'

'I don't know. Maybe he wants to make a private deal with them. Perhaps that is why he wanted to go to Deneb IV. That world is in the heart of a C area, and if he wanted to contact the Ginzoes it would be a good place to do it.'

'Yes, but Ranson, what could he gain?'

'I don't know.' The young commander stared thoughtfully at the sleeping figure of the old financier. 'He could have money worries. His wealth is based on fuel consumption, and with the slackening in interstellar trade his profits must have fallen enormously. The Terran space fleet have their own refineries, and they are the ones doing most of the space travel now. I wonder — ' His voice trailed into silence as he stared at the old man. Handley shrugged.

'I can't see it, Carl. Even if he had the crazy idea of contacting the Ginzoes, what good would it do him? Warren is a Terran, after all, he wouldn't go against his own people.'

'I wouldn't rely on that too much,' said Ranson bitterly. 'Warren wouldn't be the first man to sell out his own people for personal gain and power. Maybe I'm wrong, I hope that I am, but there's something odd about Warren, and I'd like to know just what took him to Deneb IV.'

'Then why not ask him?'

'I've tried that, it won't work. Whatever it is he intends keeping it to himself.'

'I think that you're making a mistake, Carl.' Handley stared contemptuously at the frail body of the old man. 'Warren hasn't the guts to risk his neck.'

'He did,' reminded Ranson. 'And another thing. You remember when I was bluffing him? I had him by the throat and he made a half-promise. He said: 'Let me talk to them and I'll save us all. Let me talk to them privately'. Something like that, I'm not sure of the exact words. It didn't register at the time, I had other things to think about, but I've thought of it since and I don't like the answers I get.'

'Such as?'

'Supposing Warren wanted to make a private deal with the Ginzoes? Supposing he arranged with them that his ships, or ships bearing his Insignia should have free passage? It could easily be arranged. All he would have to do would be to broadcast on a selected wavelength the identification numbers of the chosen vessels. Wouldn't that be a good idea — for Warren?'

'I see what you mean,' said Handley slowly. 'In time he would have a virtual monopoly of interstellar trade. Only his ships would be safe, and he could collect a percentage of every cargo shifted through space.'

'Exactly.'

'No.' Handley shook his head. 'It sounds nice, Carl, but it would never work. Damn it all! The Ginzoes are our enemies, they wouldn't agree to act as pirates for the benefit of one man.'

'They might if that one man gave them something worth the trouble.'

'Even so, it wouldn't work. Why, man, the Terran fleet would be suspicious. They would track it down and Warren would end in the disintegration chamber. He wouldn't have a chance of getting away with anything like that.'

'He might.' Ranson furrowed his brows with thought. 'The more I think of it, Handley, the more I am convinced that this war is a phoney war. It's lasted ten years now and after the first two there has been no real fighting. You remember the propaganda we were fed? The Ginzoes were supposed to be obscene aliens ravening for our fair worlds. They even told me once that the enemy ate the bodies of our dead. Nonsense, of course, anything grown on an oxygen planet would be deadly poison to them, but how many people know that?'

'But we are still at war, Carl. We found that out when they blasted our ship with their vortex guns.'

'Yes. They blasted us and we'd do the

same to any alien vessel approaching an O area, but is that true war? To me it seems a lot like gamekeepers protecting their rights, or patrols conserving their own areas. Another thing. If this was a real war you would think that the Terran fleet would be hungry for men and ships. I thought that. I tried to enlist and you know what happened. They didn't want me. They were satisfied with the men they had.'

'As there is no intention of taking a large scale offensive they wouldn't need many men.' Handley shifted on his bunk as he tried to follow the young man's line of reasoning. 'All they need are strong patrols around the O areas and a few ships to maintain communications with the outlying worlds.'

'Exactly.' Ranson stared at the fluorescent surface of the ceiling-plate. 'Let's make a few wild guesses and suppositions. We know that for almost three hundred years now the Terran space fleet has been an archaic leftover from the early days of history. At first they were needed, they opened up new worlds and the colonists sheltered beneath the protection of their guns. But, as time passed, and world after world was colonised without any trace of alien life, the fleet became an unnecessary expense. It still remained, of course, the burying ground of obsolete tradition, but it was of no more use than a sword was in the twentieth century wars.'

'I know that,' said Handley impatiently. 'When the hyper-drive was perfected space opened to every man with the price of a vessel. Each ship carried its own guns. Each ship was capable of a light-year-an-hour speed. The expansion was too fast, too quick for the space fleet to operate with its usual caution, and the huge warships were unwanted and un-necessary. They rotted in the ship yards or made ceremonial journeys.'

'Yes,' said Ranson quietly. 'The ships rotted — and so did the officers!'

'Did they?' Handley seemed interested. 'I didn't think that there were any left.'

'They remained on the central worlds, on Earth and the Centaurian System, policing the home planet and providing an outlet for the seekers after sinecures. Political appointments mostly, relatives and sons of the rulers and heads of state. A harmless, pleasant occupation, and no one seemed to mind the expense of keeping up an obsolete tradition. They dreamed their dreams, of course. The old dreams of military glory and supreme power, but no one minded for what harm could they do?' Ranson paused, and in the silence the sound of the old man's breathing sounded strangely loud.

'And then we discovered the Ginzoes!'

'Did we?' The engineer frowned. 'I thought that they discovered us.'

'It doesn't matter. The two races bumped into each other and immediately fear swept over Mankind. An unnecessary fear, for the aliens didn't want anything we possessed, and couldn't use it if they had it. There seemed to be no reason for war, but a frightened people do peculiar things, and someone, somewhere, saw his opportunity — and took it.'

'Do you know what you are saying, Carl?' Handley licked his dry lips. 'You'd be shot for speaking like that on Earth.'

'We're not on Earth,' said Ranson quietly. He looked at the engineer. 'It makes sense, doesn't it? Supposing that an officer, one of the old school, a man who has wasted his life in outmoded forms and empty ceremonial, suddenly saw how he could justify his existence. He wouldn't be a criminal, more likely he would be an idealist, a man wholly sincere, but blind to everything but his own ideal. He would agitate, stir up fear and worry. He would obtain a free hand and rebuild his fleet. He would bask in plaudits and feel the glow of personal power. He would send his ships into space to destroy the alien. To smash and burn this threat to Earth's supremacy — and then he would find that he couldn't do it.'

'Altair?'

'Yes, and the twenty million dead. It was a warning, Handley, and thank all the Gods of space that our man recognised it for what it was. He recognised it and felt his power slipping away and himself heading back to unwanted oblivion. He couldn't stand that. He had known what

79

it was to be important, and as long as Earth was at war he would continue to be important. Altair frightened him as it frightened every man and woman on every oxygen planet in the galaxy. He dared not continue with a full scale war, but equally so he dared not give up his power and make a truce.'

Ranson stared at the engineer. 'The answer is obvious, isn't it?'

'A phoney war?'

'Yes. A war in which the Terran space fleet had to be kept at full strength. A war in which the military would continue to be virtual dictators of the habitable worlds — but a war which could go on forever. What damage has been done to either side? A few ships have been blasted, a few men have died, trade has been handicapped and interstellar travel restricted. The great mass of the population don't even realise what is happening. They pay their taxes and imagine that the Terran space fleet is busy blasting the attacking enemy from space. Instead of which the fleets are merely guarding the approaches to the O areas and don't give a damn about carrying the war into enemy preserves.'

'It makes sense,' admitted Handley. 'It makes a lot of sense. If you are right, and you could be, then the opportunist isn't hard to find. Lasser is supreme head of military strategy. It is he who has full control of the war and has been empowered to fight it, to finish it, and to make peace. Is he the man?'

'He could be. Or there could have been a clique or cabal. They aren't villains, Handley, they are, or at least they were, sincere men who believed in what they stood for. The pity is that none of them realised that what they stood for belongs to the dark ages and the dim past. Now, with the weapons we could build and the damage we could do, total war is just another way of committing suicide. We dared not use our full powers for fear of certain retaliation, and so the war is confined to the harmless immensity of space.'

'I see, but where does Warren fit into all this?'

'Warren is a financier, a businessman,

and business men do not want war. They are the true cosmopolitans and they all speak the same language. Don't misunderstand me, Handley, I've got nothing against businessmen, they are realists and know that war is just a wanton waste. Now, with the trade routes stretching across almost the whole of the galaxy, war is something they can well do without. I think that Warren is trying to make a personal peace treaty with the Ginzoes. Once he has done it, no one is going to object too much. After all, the Terran fleet depends on taxes to keep going and the more trade, the greater the tax money will be. They would stop him now, but I don't think they would worry too much after the thing was done. That is a chance Warren would have to take, and Warren is a shrewd man.'

'But what could he offer them for free passage for his ships? What has he got that they want?' Handley stared at the young commander. 'The hyper-drive?'

'Perhaps. I don't know, but I'd like to find out.' Ranson stepped towards the sleeping man on the narrow bunk. 'I could be wrong. All this could be wild surmise, but, somehow, I don't think it is.' He shook Warren by one thin shoulder.

'What do you want?' The old man blinked in the bright lighting. 'What is it now?'

'I want to talk with you, Warren.'

'Well?'

'You're up to something, aren't you? You wanted to make a deal with the Ginzoes, and, if we hadn't been blasted, you would have done it on Deneb IV.'

'You're insane!' The old financier sat upright on the narrow bunk. 'I've never heard of anything as stupid as what you've just said.'

'I agree with you, it is stupid, but that only applies to the plan, not to the accusation. Well? Am I right?'

'Of course not.'

'Then why have you been talking to the Ginzoes while Handley and I have been sleeping? What had you to tell them that was so secret?'

'Nothing. You must be mad to even suggest it.'

'Look, Warren.' Ranson sat on the edge

of the bunk. 'Don't take me for a fool. No ordinary reason would make you leave Earth and head into a C area. You had something to do on Deneb IV, something too important to trust to anyone else. I think that you wanted to make a deal with the aliens. I still think so.'

'Well? What of it?'

'I want to be cut in.' Ranson smiled thinly down at the wrinkled features. 'Don't look so surprised, Warren. I'm a Free Trader, and I don't owe allegiance to any planet or group of planets. I'm like you, I want money, and I'm not too particular just how I get it.'

'You make a poor liar, Ranson.' Warren stared at the young commander, and the expression in his pale blue eyes was one of pitying contempt. 'Do you think that you can bluff me like that? Why, man, I've operated in the money marts of a dozen worlds, operated against experts. Do you even imagine that I would be fooled by an ignorant space rat?'

'So you admit it?'

'I admit nothing. What do your childish accusations mean to me?' Warren laughed, a soft, dry chuckling, and his thin lips writhed into a sneer. 'You have amused me, Ranson. It is easy for an old man to feign sleep, and your excellent discourse on the history of the war amused me more than you could ever guess. Incidentally, it may please you to know that you were perfectly correct. Lasser did seize his opportunity, and, backed by certain individuals who shall remain nameless, did exaggerate the threat of the Ginzo invasion. But you were wrong on one thing. We are after more than continuation of a phoney war. More than the dribbling amounts of tax money to enable us to keep a few ships operating in space. The prize is bigger than that, Ranson. Much bigger.'

'Then it was all true.' Handley stared at the young commander. 'You guessed right, Carl.'

'Yes.' Ranson nodded and turned to the old man. 'But I didn't guess far enough. There is more in this than I imagined.' He stepped towards the financier. 'You used the term 'we', Warren. That was a mistake, I think.' He lifted his hands, the fingers curved to fit a scrawny throat.

'Talk, Warren! Talk, or die!'

'You fool!' There was no mistaking the contempt in the old man's whispering tones. 'You think to threaten me? Touch me, and you die.' He relaxed, smiling up at the young commander. 'You are too late, Ranson. The thing is done. I have contacted the aliens and now the Ginzoes and I are allies. If you harm me they will kill you — and the manner of your death will be such as to make men shudder at the memory.'

'Talk,' snapped Ranson. 'Empty talk. But you are dangerous, Warren. As dangerous as a mad dog, and, like a mad dog, you should be eliminated.'

He surged forward, his hands lunging for the old man's throat, then stiffened, his eyes widening in shocked unbelief as he stared at the glinting thing in Warren's hand.

'A flare-gun!' He teetered a little, poised on the balls of his feet. 'Where did you get it?'

'Does that matter?' Warren lifted the heavy weapon, centring the pitted orifice directly on the young man's stomach. 'I warned you, Ranson. I told you what would happen if you touched me. Now I am going to kill you. I am going to burn your stomach to ash and leave you to crawl on the stumps of your legs until you die!'

Slowly his finger tightened around the trigger.

6

Catalyst of death

Ranson stared at the pitted orifice of the weapon, his stomach muscles tightening against the expected blast of energy. His senses seemed to have become unnaturally sharp, his time awareness speeded so that he watched the whitening knuckle of the old man, the swollen firing chamber of the flare-gun, the cooling vanes and the knurled butt, as if from the viewpoint of an uninterested observer. Then he felt his body falling, lunging towards the menacing gun, and he knew that his automatic reflexes had taken over.

Too late.

He was too far from the old man. Too far from the pointing weapon, and even as he dived forward he cringed to the heat and agony of the anticipated flare-gun charge. Warren's finger had to move five millimetres to trigger the weapon, while he had to cover two metres of distance in the same period of time. He couldn't do it. No man could do it. No man could escape the electronic speed of a flare-gun charge when the gunner's finger was already squeezing the trigger. It only needed a touch and a shaft of ravening energy would lance from the pitted orifice, thundering with the fury of exploding atoms, searing and burning everything in its path,

Warren grinned as he aimed the gun, his thin finger pressing the trigger, his pale blue eyes glittering with emotion and blood-lust.

Nothing happened!

No lancing flame. No thundering discharge. No searing heat or blistering energy. The gun clicked, clicked again as the old man desperately squeezed the trigger, then Ranson was gripping a thin wrist and Warren screamed with fear and pain.

'Drop it!' The young commander kicked the weapon towards the engineer. 'So you'd kill me, would you, Warren? You'd shoot me down like a dog. Why?'

'Leave me alone!' Hate and rage made the old financier's features horrible to look upon. 'The Ginzoes will get you for this. Let me alone!'

'Not until you talk, Warren. Where did you get the flare-gun? Answer me, damn you! Where did you get it?'

'They gave it to me. I asked for it. I was afraid of you.' Warren jerked his words with a breathless haste. 'Don't hurt me, Ranson. I wouldn't have shot you. I swear it!'

'He's speaking the truth,' said Handley drily. He held the weapon in his hand and stared down at it with a puzzled expression. 'Though he doesn't know it. He couldn't have shot you. Not with this, anyway.'

'Why not?'

'It isn't loaded. That's why.' The big man threw the weapon on to a bunk with a contemptuous snort. 'Fancy trying to kill a man with an unchecked gun! You should have had more sense. Warren.'

'I didn't know — ' babbled the old man. Then cringed at Ranson's expression. 'Don't look at me like that. I'm an old man. I'm not well. Don't hurt me, Ranson. Don't hurt me!'

'I should kill you as I'd kill vermin!' Ranson released the thin wrist and threw the old man hard against the metal wall. 'I will kill you if you don't talk and talk fast. What is this all about?'

'You were right.' Warren rubbed his scrawny wrist and some of the fear left his pale blue eyes. 'There is a cabal and their object is supreme power. Not just a continuation of the war, but real power. A military dictatorship with absolute rule over every oxygen planet in the galaxy. You could be a part of it, Ranson. Help me now, and I'll see that you are given full Governorship over an entire System. Think of it, man! You'd have more power than any despot of old. More power than any king or emperor! You'd be rich beyond the dreams of avarice and your slightest word would be law. Well?'

'Words,' sneered the Free Trader. 'Empty words without meaning. I've heard wild dreams before, Warren. Heard them a thousand times on a hundred worlds.'

'This is more than just words. I'm not a fool, Ranson, but I am an ambitious man. I know Lasser. I helped him to power, several of us did, and now is the time for our reward.' The old man hunched forward on the narrow bunk. 'Listen. You are a shrewd devil, Ranson, you extrapolated the truth from a few facts and some imaginative thinking. The war is a phoney war. The Ginzoes came at just the right time, and we've used them to support a growing space fleet. I'll admit that at first Lasser was sincere. He really believed that there could be no room for two intelligent races in the same galaxy, but Altair changed his mind. He could blast the Ginzo planets, but then they would blast ours. For a few days there was a danger of peace, but then I and others like me stepped into the picture and Lasser changed his mind.'

'You offered — '

'Supreme power!' Something flared in the pale blue eyes, and Warren licked his thin lips with a cat-like, almost feral gesture. 'I saw the chance and we took it. The one chance this civilization could ever offer for personal, absolute power. We made our plans, cunning, foolproof plans, and now we are ready to declare the new order. There will be an end of popular rule. There will be an end of elections and representatives, of slow legislation and worry about the rights of the individual. Now the old regime will return. One man, one brain, one will and one law. Now will dawn the Empire of Space!'

'He's crazy,' whispered Handley and, staring at the old man, Ranson had to agree. The sere features writhed and tiny specks of foam clung to the corners of the thin lips. The pale blue eyes blazed with burning ambition and the wrinkled skin flushed beneath the surge of blood. Warren was in the grip of an overpowering, fanatical emotion, and Ranson knew that the old man was speaking the literal truth.

'We can do it,' whispered Warren, and his dry tones carried an insane form of ecstasy. 'We have the power and we shall rule. It is our destiny!'

'You'll never get away with it.' Ranson

shuddered, as he stared at the distorted features of the old financier. 'As soon as you set up your dictatorship the people will rise and cut you down. Why, man, you'd need an army of billions to occupy the oxygen worlds, and even then you'd never be safe. The galaxy is too big for any one group to rule as you want to rule. There are too many hyper-drive ships, too many forms of transport, and too many atomic weapons lined up against you. No, Warren. Your dream will end like all the others — in a gutter or with a rope around your neck!'

'You think so?' Warren shrugged. 'Tell me, Ranson. Would you obey me?'

'No.'

'Would you try to kill me?'

'If you set up your dictatorship? Yes.'

'Would you kill or disobey me if you knew that the penalty would be the destruction of the oxygen worlds?' Warren leaned forward and the madness had gone from his eyes, leaving them clear and intelligent. Ranson shrugged.

'You are stating a supposition,' he said flatly, 'No man would be insane enough to destroy a planet because he was disobeyed. And equally so, no man would carry out the order. You would be bluffing — and how long do you think that bluff would last?'

'It would be no bluff,' said Warren grimly. 'I know that, and the people will know it, too. Our regime will be safeguarded as no other has ever been. The rulers will be absolute despots and they will remain so for all time. Any attempt at assassination. Any rebellion or refusal to obey will result in the death of a world. Would you risk that penalty?'

'No, but while you depend on humans to carry out your orders, you can never be safe. Men who would contemplate the destruction of a world are few, and for every one found there are ten million to stop him.'

'But suppose that it did not rest on a man? Suppose that it rested on an alien?' Warren leaned even closer, and Ranson felt his muscles tense as he realised what the old man was saying.

'You mean?'

'Supposing the power to destroy were

given, not to a man, but to an alien. What then?'

'No!' Ranson shook his head and he heard Handley's hissing inhalation as the engineer gripped his arm.

'Why not?' Warren leaned back and his smile was something straight from the lowermost regions of hell. 'I know that we could never trust a man to do what must be done. Any man would hesitate, would be open to murder or bribery, would think, and think, and then think again. A man, Ranson — but not an alien. They would have no interest in bribes. They would do no more than carry out a promise, a promise incidentally which would give them a usable planet, and they would think no more of it than you would if you killed a fly.'

'You devil!' Handley surged forward and grunted as Ranson jabbed his elbow deep into his stomach.

'Hold it!' snapped the young commander. 'Let him finish!'

'I have finished.' Warren twisted his thin lips in a triumphant smile. 'The plan is finished. The weapon has been completed and now we shall take over.'

'Impossible! You've been with us all the time. You couldn't have contacted anyone, unless — ' He paled, and Handley grunted as they realised the truth.

'Yes,' said Warren calmly. 'Who else? The aliens, who are to hold the one weapon which will bring every man and woman in the galaxy to their knees are — the Ginzoes.' He screamed with sudden fear as Handley lunged for his throat.

'Stop it!' Ranson jerked at the engineer's thick wrists. 'Damn you, Handley, let him live. I want to talk to him.'

Handley snarled as his big hands tightened around the scrawny throat. Ranson took one look at the mottled features of the old man, at the starting eyes and swelling tongue, then his hand swept in a vicious arc and the stiffened edge of his palm slammed the big engineer at the base of the neck.

He fell in an untidy heap, falling as a pole-axed animal falls, like a felled tree. Ranson caught him as he slumped towards the metal deck plates, then, anxiously felt the big man's pulse and began to massage his neck.

'What hit me?' Handley grunted and winced as he rubbed the base of his skull. 'Carl! Why did you stop me?'

'Time enough to kill him if we have to. Now I want to talk to him, there are things we must learn before we decide.' He stared thoughtfully at the gasping figure of the old man, 'Personally, I think that he's just bluffing, No such weapon can exist.'

'You think not?' Warren showed his yellow teeth in an animal-snarl. 'Don't be too certain of that. It does exist, and the Ginzoes have knowledge of it. Be careful how you treat me, Ranson. I hold your life and the lives of all men in the hollow of my hand.'

'Bluff!'

'You think so?' Warren shrugged and when he spoke again his voice was surprisingly calm. 'What are the seas made of, Ranson? What is in the ocean of every oxygen world? I'll tell you. Oxygen, hydrogen, some rare earths, some minerals, a trace of radioactives — and salt. Salt, Ranson. Billions of tons of salt! Do you know what salt is? Sodium chloride! Do you know what happens when you pass an electric current through saline?'

'I know,' said Ranson tightly, and his arm ached from the effort of restraining the big engineer.

'A gas is liberated, Ranson. A thick, green-yellow gas. Chlorine! Now do you understand?'

'You wouldn't dare!'

'Imagine a catalyst. A handful of crystals. Special crystals, Ranson. Very special. A Ginzo ship sweeps down from outer space, passes over a sea and drops those crystals into the ocean. The catalyst will not wear out it will continue to operate without loss to itself working quietly in the depths of the sea, unnoticed, undiscoverable — unstoppable. A simple thing, really. It does what an electric current would do. It breaks down the sodium chloride into its basic elements and liberates — chlorine!'

'You're mad,' breathed Ranson sickly. 'To even think of such a thing.'

'Men would hesitate at using such a weapon. Men would shrink at spoiling a world, but aliens — ' Warren laughed and the sound of his laughter rang hollowly from the bare metal walls. 'The Ginzoes are chlorine breathers. Would they hesitate? Would they stop at converting an oxygen world into a chlorine one? I think not, Ranson. I think that they would welcome the chance to use it, and they will, unless the race of man bows at the feet of its new rulers!'

'No!' Ranson wiped at the sweat streaming from his face and neck. 'We're at war with the Ginzoes. You couldn't have been mad enough to give them such a weapon. Why, man! They can plant that stuff in every sea and within a few years we'd all be just a memory on the scroll of time. No, Warren. Power just isn't worth what you intend. Even the dream of absolute rule over an entire galaxy isn't worth the murder of an entire race.'

'You think not?' Warren smiled, and then, with shocking abruptness, his wrinkled features writhed and altered.

'What do I care for scum? What do the lives of ignorant rabble mean to me? For power, I would climb on the living bodies of a trillion men. I exist only for myself, Ranson. I am I, and if you wish you may serve me.'

'No,' said the young commander quietly. 'I'll not serve you.' His grey eyes held pity as he stared at the contorted features of the old man. 'You are ill, Warren. You've lived with a dream for too long and now you confuse dreams with reality. There is no catalyst. There will be no Empire of Space. You know it. You know that it cannot be done, and that even if it could you would not do it.'

'Fool!' Anger, hate, and a peculiar sadistic gloating rang in the old man's whispering voice. 'The thing is done! A touch of gas, the Ginzoes are excellent chemists, and we conferred while you slept. I have given them the weapon. A simple formula, simple enough for an old man to remember. I gave it to them and they gave me the flare-gun as promise that they would keep their bargain. They will not use the catalyst unless ordered by the rulers of the oxygen worlds.'

He frowned, a questioning look replacing the insane glare in his pale blue eyes.

'They gave me a gun,' he whispered. 'But they didn't load it for me — ' He looked up and fear twisted his wrinkled face into a grotesque mask.

'No! Ranson, save me' Help! Help!'

'Stop it!' Ranson grabbed at the engineer. 'Take it easy! Handley!'

On the bunk the old man cowered and the sound of his screams echoed from the bare metal of the room. Ranson cursed, grabbed at the engineer, missed, swung his fist, then staggered back at the thrust of a huge arm.

'You'll die!' raved Warren. 'You'll all die! Touch me and the planets will suffer for it. Help!'

'Damn you!' Handley grabbed at the shrieking man, 'So you'd sell us out, would you? You'd give us all over to the enemy. All of us. Men and women, babies and little children. You'd kill us all just so as you could sit on a gilded throne and play at being a king. Well, damn you, you'll never live to see it.'

His big hands moved, gripped, twisted — and Warren's screams died with the snap of his broken neck. Dully the big man stared down at the crumpled figure on the narrow bunk, and when he finally moved it was as if he walked through water or clinging sand.

'I've killed him,' he muttered. 'I've killed the swine.'

'Yes,' said Ranson grimly. 'You've killed him. Now, if he spoke the truth, the Ginzoes will revenge his death. They will kill us, then they will drop the catalyst on an oxygen world.' He stared curiously at the other. 'How does it feel to have murdered a world, Handley? Was killing Warren worth it?'

'Don't!' pleaded the big man. 'I couldn't stand it any longer, Carl. To stand there and hear him talk like that. I — ' He shuddered and buried his face in his hands.

'Forget it,' said Ranson gently. 'I'm not blaming you, but I wish that you had waited. He didn't deserve such a clean death.'

He tensed, frowning, his muscles tightening at a familiar sound, and even as he heard it his nostrils quivered to the tell-tale scent of chlorine.

He knew what to expect before he turned to face the wall containing the airlock, and he stood, tight-lipped staring at what stood within the vestibule beyond the open panel.

The Ginzoes had arrived — too late, and Warren welcomed them with his grimacing smile of dying fear.

Slowly they entered the room.

7

Fifty days to doom

There were three of them this time. Three suited figures and before them they pushed the inevitable, instrument-loaded trolley. One of the aliens carried a shapeless bundle, while on the small conveyor, in addition to the communication instruments, rested what seemed to be a bowl of water.

Silently they spread themselves before the open panel and Ranson stepped forward, his throat dry with fear.

'Yes?'

The machine clicked and hummed then, with its inhuman drone, spilled words into the silence of the room.

'One of you has been destroyed.'

It was a statement, not a question, and the young commander didn't trouble to deny it.

'Yes.'

'Why was he destroyed?'

'He betrayed us. He deserved to die.'

'Why?'

Ranson cursed the cold logic of the aliens and the impossibility of translating emotion into mutually understandable symbols.

'He was inefficient,' he said. 'It was better that he should not remain a member of my group.'

'We understand.' The machine clicked and fell silent as the aliens communicated with the others in the ship. Ranson hoped that they would accept his explanation and sweated as he remembered what Warren had screamed just before he died. The machine hummed and its inhuman drone echoed from the bare walls of the room.

'The one destroyed did not belong to your group. He was a group different to yours. Why did you kill him?'

'He tried to kill me,' snapped Ranson savagely. 'That's why.'

'Destroy you?'

'Yes, damn you. With the flare-gun you let him have in return for his secret.'

'The weapon was ineffective.'

'I know it — now.' The young man frowned at the machine. 'Why did you give him an empty flare-gun?'

'He asked for a weapon. He did not say anything about charges for it.'

'What?' Ranson stared at the suited aliens, then, as understanding came. Doubled in a fit of helpless laughter. 'You knew!' he gasped. 'You and your damn logic. You knew all the time!'

'Knew what?' Handley stepped forward and glowered at the Ginzoes. 'What goes on here, Carl?'

'Don't you get it, Handley?' Ranson fought his hysterical outburst. 'Warren asked for a gun. They gave him exactly what he asked for, but, as he didn't ask for a loaded weapon, they didn't give him one. Obviously, they knew what he wanted it for.' He stared at the aliens with increasing respect; 'You know,' he said slowly. 'I'm beginning to like the Ginzoes.'

'Like them!'

'Yes. They don't want this war any more than we do, and by 'we' I mean the

average person. Also, and this is important, they seem to have a peculiar sense of
humour. They're coldly logical, of course,
but even so, they do reveal one of the
saving graces of Terrans. I'll bet that in a
way they are laughing at us.'

'Don't be too sure of that,' said the
engineer grimly. 'You're basing that
assumption on insufficient data. They
may not have intended anything when
they gave Warren that gun. Suppose that
he had asked for a loaded weapon? Where
would you be now?'

'Dead,' admitted Ranson soberly. 'You're
right, Handley. The Ginzoes are still our
enemies — and we mustn't forget it.'

The machine clicked and droned and
in the silence of the room the mechanical
sound seemed to be charged with a subtle
menace.

'We have kept you. You have agreed to
help us. Do you still agree?'

'Yes.' Ranson stared at the suited figures
and frowned as he tried to remember
whether or not he spoke to the original
questioner. He shrugged, the aliens seemed
all the same, and, to them, he supposed

108

all Terrans looked alike. Yet something about the questions, something about the easy use of words and the lack of stilted Terran gave him a clue.

'You sent for an experienced speaker,' he said. 'While we waited here you have added a being skilled in our language, and used to operating the communication machines. Is that so?'

'Yes.'

'Why?'

'It was necessary. The one who has been destroyed could not make himself understood to those aboard the vessel. He had vital information to impart. Very vital.'

'And did he?' Ranson stared at the machine, half-hoping that Warren had died before he could reveal the secret of the catalyst, half-hoping that the old man had tried a colossal bluff. The droning machine put an end to his hopes.

'He did.'

'I see.' Ranson glanced at the engineer. 'What was it that he told you?'

'He gave us the information which will enable us to end the war forever.' The

109

mechanical voice could not portray emotion, but Ranson could imagine the satisfaction behind the droning words. Beside him Handley grunted and stepped forward, his big fists clenched and his broad features tense and savage.

'We've got to get that information, Carl. If they ever use it — ' He swallowed and stepped nearer to the silent aliens and the droning machine.

'Hold it, Handley!' Ranson caught the big man by the arm. 'Killing them wouldn't do us any good, and if we tried it we'd be dead before we could reach them. Warren spoke the truth, he did give them the secret of the catalyst, and there's nothing we can do about it.'

'Isn't there?' Handley growled deep in his chest. 'They may not have broadcast the information yet. If we get these Ginzoes, take the ship — '

'Impossible! Besides, why should we worry? We both know that Warren was bluffing. No such catalyst can exist as the one he described.' Ranson sweated as he stared at the watchful aliens. 'He was desperate to save his life and would have promised anything. An old man like him wouldn't have any idea as to what he was saying. Forget it.'

'Yeah.' Handley gulped and relaxed as he grasped the meaning of what the young commander hoped to do. 'He was a crazy old coot, anyway. What would he know of chemistry?'

It was useless. Ranson knew it, but something deep within him refused to let him ignore the slightest chance of deluding the aliens. If they could give the impression that Warren had been insane, that his frenzied babbling was the product of a diseased mind, then maybe, just maybe, the Ginzoes would ignore the supposed catalyst.

Maybe!

'You are members of a strange race,' droned the machine, and if a man had been talking Ranson would have guessed the words to be ironic. 'A very strange race. You are egotistical, emotional, illogical, and immature. You insist on waging a war that can serve no useful purpose, a war that must be crippling your economy with its expenditure of energy. Why is that so?'

'We don't want war,' said Ranson tightly. 'Not the bulk of the population. Only a small group desire to continue this useless struggle, but they are in power and the rest follow where they lead,'

'Could you not destroy the unit which has proved itself to be unreliable?'

'No.'

'Why not?'

'I can't answer that.' Ranson stared bleakly at the droning machine. 'We haven't words in common for me to tell you. How can I describe hate and fear? How can I make you understand that most of the Terran population live in dread of you? They don't really hate you, but they are afraid that one day your ships may sweep from outer space and destroy their worlds. They fear you, and fearing you, they hate you. To us there can be only one answer to hate. We must destroy you. Blast you from the galaxy before you blast us. That is the reason why the power-group can remain in authority. That is the reason for the continuation of the war.'

'Is it?' Almost it seemed as if the operating Ginzo shrugged. 'We learned differently from the one you destroyed. He spoke of a small group imposing its will on the majority. He stated that the war was merely an excuse for those in power to remain in command. He bargained with us and promised us many new chlorine worlds for our use. Did he speak truth?'

'Yes,' said Ranson dully, and hated himself for belonging to the same race as Warren. 'He spoke truth.'

'Then the catalyst was no raving of an insane mind.'

'I don't know. I have never heard of such a substance. I daren't think that it could exist.'

'It does,' droned the machine, and one of the aliens stepped forward, something small and bright glistening at the tip of one tentacle. It hovered over the bowl of water, fell — and thick clouds of green-yellow gas streamed from the surface of the bowl.

'The catalyst,' droned the machine. 'Watch!'

'It works! By God, it works!' Handley lunged forward, then staggered back, his breath rasping in his throat from the effects of the poison. 'Ranson! Warren was right!'

'Yes.' Ranson stared sombrely at the mounting clouds of chlorine rising from the smooth surface of the water. 'He was right — and he has given the fate of Mankind into the keeping of an alien race!'

Suddenly he wanted to be sick.

It was the end. The end of the ten-year struggle for the dominance of space. With the catalyst the Ginzoes could convert every oxygen world in the galaxy to a chlorine one — and man would be finished! He clenched his fists until the nails dug into the palms of his hands and cursed Warren and all he stood for with a savage violence. Greed for power. The selfish, short-sighted lust for the glittering baubles of empire and personal ambition had driven the old man to sell out the race of man. Now? He swallowed as he tried to imagine what would happen if the positions were reversed. If the Terrans had a weapon capable of subduing the Ginzoes, would they use it? Or would they retain it as an argument for peace? He didn't know, but he remembered the cultivated war-hysteria and patriotic frenzy that had swept the oxygen worlds at the declaration of war, and he knew, too, the emotional frailty of men.

Dully he became aware of the droning of the communication machine.

'You made a promise. You offered to serve us if we would keep you. Now is the time for you to carry out your bargain.'

'What's the use,' he said with savage bitterness. 'What do you need the hyper-drive for — now? With that catalyst you can ruin the oxygen worlds and have complete dominance over the entire galaxy. I take back my offer. Kill me if you like, but Terrans have done enough damage to their own kind, and I'm damned if I'm going to do more.'

'You misunderstand,' droned the machine, and again Ranson imagined a hidden emotion in the mechanical words. 'We do not intend to destroy your worlds. Such wanton destruction of intelligent life is contrary to the Great Design. There is room and to spare for both races — but this senseless war must be ended.'

'I agree. But how?'

'We can ruin your worlds. You can blast our planets with your weapons, but of what use will that be to you when your own worlds are rendered useless? Where will you go? What will you do when your seas begin emitting the chlorine that is poison to you? Once we use the catalyst there will not be a single planet in the galaxy capable of supporting your kind of life. We may suffer, but we will survive. You will not survive. You will be eliminated.'

'So you are going to use it.' Ranson swallowed as he fought the rising sickness in his stomach. 'You damn, inhuman swine!'

'No. We are not to blame. It was one of your own groups who gave us the weapon. Are we to blame for considering its use?'

'No,' admitted Ranson. 'You are alien and you are at war. Perhaps you are not to blame. Not now. But will you sleep easy in your beds knowing that you have destroyed an entire race? Perhaps you will, I don't know, but I do know that no intelligent mind could remember such a crime and remain wholly sane,'

'We said that we considered its use,' reminded the droning machine, and Ranson stared at the suited aliens in sudden hope.

'Then — ' He swallowed and tried to steady his voice. 'Then you don't intend using it?'

'We did not say that. It may be that we shall have to use it. Not willingly, perhaps, but if necessary we shall. It rests with your own race.'

'How?'

'This war must stop. It is draining our energy, energy that we need for other purposes, and it is an illogical struggle. We shall retain the catalyst, but if your race is as intelligent as we think, it will never be used.'

'Well?' Ranson sweated with impatience. 'What have we got to do?'

'You are to carry an ultimatum to your people. Peace must be declared. The star lanes must be open for all. We must be left alone to go our own way on our own worlds, and both races must live, if not in friendship, at least in harmony. We are tired of this stupid conflict, and, unless it is halted, we shall exterminate your race!'

'Then why don't you radio to Earth? Tell the High Command what you intend. Lasser will have no option but to end the war.'

'No.' Almost Ranson could imagine one of the aliens shaking his head. 'That would prove nothing but that the war had ended through fear of our race. You have already explained what happens when your own people fear something. They destroy it. We do not wish to live in constant watchfulness against sudden attack.'

'Then — '

'You will contact your leading group. You will tell them what has occurred. You will explain to them what they must do.'

'But that is exactly the same thing,' protested Ranson. 'What does it matter how the war is ended just as long as peace is declared?'

'You have claimed to be an intelligent race,' droned the machine. 'As yet we have had no proof of that. This is your chance to prove to us that you should be tolerated. Surely it would be a simple thing for you to inform your leading group of the catalyst? They, if they are intelligent, will realise that the war must end. We ask nothing from you. We offer nothing. But, if, even after knowing what must inevitably happen, if the war is pursued, your leading group does not declare a peace, then we shall not hesitate. The Great Design forbids the destruction of intelligent life, but, any race that cannot see the obvious must be classed as vermin — and we have no compunction against the elimination of vermin.'

'So I'm to tell them that unless they declare peace you will use the catalyst.' Ranson nodded. 'Right. Now, how do I get to Earth?'

'You are now on a world which we have used for the storage of captured vessels and prisoners. The ship is an old one, but you said that you could repair your faster-than-light unit. You will do so. You will leave this system and contact your leading group. You will tell them what has happened here and what they must do.'

'Can't you give me a workable vessel?' Ranson wiped his streaming face and neck. 'The sooner this is over the better.'

'You will do as you promised,' droned the mechanical voice. 'We are weary of your race. Now we have decided to make an end one way or another. The future of your race depends on you. Unless you can repair the vessel and convey the message then we must judge you to be incompetent and unnecessary.'

'I see.' The young commander shrugged. 'Fair enough. How much time have I got?'

'Unless peace has been declared within fifty rotations of your home planet we shall use the catalyst.'

'Fifty days!' Ranson glanced at the engineer.

'Is that all? Supposing something goes wrong?'

'That is your concern,' droned the cold voice. 'Your vessel will bear markings safeguarding it from our war-ships. We shall not fire on you or hinder you in any way, but, peace must be declared within the period stated or it will be too late.'

The machine clicked with a grim finality, and silence filled the bare metal room.

In the silence the clash of metal striking metal sounded strangely loud, and Ranson stared at the bundle one of the aliens had thrown to the deck plates. He stooped over it, opening it out, and staring at the two space suits with expert eyes. Rapidly he checked the air tanks and oxygen hissed from the open valve. He twisted it shut and glanced at the engineer.

'They want us to put these things on and leave the ship.' He thinned his lips as he looked towards the waiting Ginzoes. 'Hurry it up, Handley. We've only got fifty days to save our entire race.'

Suddenly his hands began to tremble and his stomach knotted as full realisation came.

Fifty days to save Mankind!

Numbly he began to don the space suit.

8

Delila

The ship had gone. The strange, alien vessel with its crew of Ginzoes and the solitary body of a dead Terran.

It had whooshed up into space and disappeared into a clear blue sky bearing with it the terrible secret that threatened half the galaxy with extinction. It had left with a flare of rockets and a surging tumult of displaced air, and Ranson had been glad to see it go.

He stood, the space suit a crumpled mass at his feet, and breathed gratefully at the clean, fragrant air of a strange oxygen planet. Before him stretched the rolling green sward of fertile land. Behind him a river gurgled as it raced towards an unknown sea, and small trees and flowering shrubs dotted the bright green of the rolling plain.

On that plain rested what seemed to be

an engineer's nightmare.

A ship reared its scarred nose towards the clear blue of the sky. Around it, thrown in careless confusion, were heaped bales and boxes, coils of wire and glistening components, the sagging ruin of a dozen hyper-drive units and racks of tools and equipment. It was the gathered ruin of a dozen gutted vessels and it rested beneath the blue of the sky like a spilt box of mechanical toys.

'There's our ship,' said Ranson grimly. 'All we have to do is to repair it, find out just where we are, get to Earth, contact Lasser, make him declare peace, and make sure that the Ginzoes understand. All within fifty days. Can we do it, Handley?'

'It depends on the state of the ship.' The engineer grunted as his experienced eyes scanned the scarred vessel. 'Look at it! That type hasn't been seen in the space lanes for over fifty years now. The design was obsolete before I was born. They must have found it in a museum.'

'They seem to have given us plenty of spares and equipment.' Ranson kicked at the grass as they walked towards the jumble of boxes. 'They must have used this planet as a dumping ground.'

'Let's hope that we can use some of it,' said Handley grimly. 'If they took it all from ships blasted by their vortex guns it will be useless. Look at those hyper-drive units! You can see that they are just so much scrap metal from here. If the rest of the ship is like that — ' He shrugged and Ranson knew just what the big man meant. Once a vessel had been caught in the fire of a Ginzo vortex gun everything electrical on it was wrecked, and, if they had nothing better to work with, Mankind was as good as dead.

Tensely they began to examine the heaped supplies.

'It could be worse,' grunted Handley, after a while. 'The tools are good, some of the components and there is quite a stack of thermocans. We won't go hungry for a while, at any rate.' He straightened his back and squinted his eyes at the setting sun. 'I wonder what planet this is? I'd have thought that there would have been settlers here, the climate seems perfect.'

'Probably some out of the way planet, maybe one that hasn't been discovered yet. The galaxy is a big place, Handley, and even with the hyper-drive it takes time to colonise every suitable world.' Ranson wiped sweat from his streaming forehead and stared at the ship. 'One thing's certain, that ship has been here for quite a while.'

'What makes you say that?'

'Look at how the earth has collected at the base. The grass is quite high and there are no signs of landing scars.' He frowned in sudden thought. 'The Ginzoes said that they had dumped prisoners here, too. I wonder where they are?'

'Does it matter?' Handley shrugged as he stooped to examine the strained bulk of a hyper-drive unit. We can do without them. Anyway, unless we can get this crate into space it won't matter much. The Ginzoes are certain to seed this planet with the catalyst.'

He stooped even lower over the warped casing, his eyes narrowed as he peered at the distorted coils and the cracked supports. He grunted, reached for a tool, then yelled as something droned through the air and exploded against the thick metal of the unit.

'Carl. Get down!'

'Why?' The young commander stared at the big man then dropped as something flared against the hull of the ship. 'What's happening?'

'Someone's shooting at us, that's what.' Cautiously the engineer peered towards a small clump of trees.

'Dammit! I wish I had a flare-gun!' He winced as incandescent vapour seared his bare hand.

'High velocity slugs!' Ranson hugged the ground as he crawled towards the big man. 'Someone is using an HV rifle. If one of those slugs hits either of us anywhere on the limbs or body the hydrostatic shock will kill faster than a flare-gun. Keep down, Handley.'

'What do you think I'm doing?' The big man grunted as one of the tiny missiles vented its kinetic energy in a rush of incandescent vapour as it struck the unyielding metal of the hyper-drive unit. 'There's a sniper over in those trees. What shall we do, Carl? We can't stay here, and with what we've got to do we daren't chance getting shot.'

'I know that,' said Ranson grimly, and there was a sound of ripping fabric as he tore the blouse from his shoulders. 'Hey, there! You!' He waved the blouse above his head. 'Quit firing! We're Terrans, I tell you. Terrans from Earth! Quit firing!'

Three shots tore the blouse from his hand and the sound of the distant rifle echoed spitefully across the plain.

'The crazy fool!' Handley reddened with anger. 'If I could get my hands on him I'd pulp his neck!' He stared worriedly at the young commander. 'Now what? He didn't seem to recognise your signal.'

'It must be a man out there,' said Ranson tightly. 'He can keep us bottled up here forever, especially if he's using an infra-red viewer on his rifle.' He gnawed at his lower lip. 'We can't stay here, not when time is so important. I'm going to take a chance.'

'What sort of a chance?' Handley swore as the young man rose deliberately to his feet. 'Carl! Are you crazy? That sniper can't miss!'

'That's what I'm hoping.' Ranson flinched as a bullet droned past his ear. 'Keep where you are, Handley. I've an idea that our friend doesn't want to kill us. He could have dropped us both while we were examining the supplies, but instead of that he's been throwing lead all around us.' He stared towards the trees and slowly raised both hands in the universal gesture of peace.

The rifle fell silent.

'We're Terrans,' called Ranson. 'Friends.'

'Yeah?' The voice echoed from the clump of trees, a peculiar, high-pitched voice. 'Where's the other one?'

'Stand up, Handley,' ordered Ranson. 'Show yourself.' He waited until the big man had risen to his feet. 'That's the lot,' he shouted. 'There were only two of us.'

'I know it,' drawled the voice. 'Now turn around, face the ship, and keep your hands above your heads. I'm coming out.'

Slowly they did as ordered and waited, little chills running up their spines, for the mysterious marksman to show himself.

'All right, you. Turn around. Steady now, remember that I've a rifle covering the two of you.'

Tensely Ranson turned, and, as his eyes focussed on the sniper, he heard Handley's muttered curse.

'A woman!'

He was right.

She stood before them, a tall, loose-limbed girl in her early twenties. A mane of glinting blonde hair swept from her forehead and fell to her shoulders, the thick tresses confined in a strip of brightly coloured ribbon. She wore high boots and slacks, a man's shirt and a wide leather belt. The hilt of a knife showed above the belt, and she carried a long barrelled rifle with familiar ease. She stared at them coldly with her bright blue eyes and her tanned skin flushed a little.

'Well?'

'What's the idea of shooting at us?' Ranson tried to control his anger. 'Didn't you know that we were Terrans?'

'Didn't know and didn't care. Strangers aren't wanted here, mister. I just thought I'd teach you a lesson. Come near the Ship again and I'll drill you between the eyes.'

'This is crazy!' Ranson stared at the girl and moved a little closer. 'Who are you? One of the prisoners?'

'Prisoner?' The girl shrugged. 'They call me Delila, and I'm no prisoner. This is my spell at watch over the Ship.' She glanced at the setting sun. 'Now, move, and keep on moving, or I'll drill you!'

'Wait!' Ranson licked his lips. 'We were dumped here by the Ginzoes. You know of them?'

'No.'

'Damn it, you must do! We aren't the only Terrans that have been dumped here. Where are the others?'

'In the woods, I guess. I wouldn't know. We shoot a few of 'em now and again when they try to raid the Ship.'

'Yeah? Who's 'we'?'

'Us, the owners of this planet.' She stared coldly at the young man. 'Don't you know the Word?'

'What word?'

'That means that you don't know it.' She gestured with the rifle. 'Get moving now. Before I change my mind and shoot you both.'

'Wait!' Ranson narrowed his eyes at a furtive movement behind the young woman, then, as he realized what it was, continued talking. 'We've only just landed here. We're hungry, unarmed, tired. Can't you take us to your village and let us get some rest?'

'Move!'

'Take it easy,' growled the big engineer. 'That's no way to talk to visitors.'

'Look, mister,' she said tightly. 'You can walk or you can die. Which is it to be?' Suddenly the rifle was menacing them with its tiny orifice and her finger whitened as she squeezed the trigger. Handley gulped.

'We'll move,' he said, and slowly walked towards the girl.

'Stop!' She stepped backwards, the long barrel of the rifle jerking from Ranson to the engineer. 'Not that way! Walk to your right, away from me and away from the Ship.' The rifle gestured. 'You too, mister. Get moving!'

'Yes,' said Ranson, and stumbled as he

took a long stride. He staggered, almost fell, and the girl sprang backward, away from his outstretched arms. She glared at him, her eyes glinting like twin pools of frozen oxygen, and the rifle in her hands steadied as she levelled the barrel.

'Right, mister,' she snapped. 'You asked for it!'

Fire spat from the muzzle as she squeezed the trigger, and with the spiteful crack of the weapon came her startled scream.

Ranson grunted as he rose from the soft dirt. He brushed at sticky blades of grass then, with cold indifference, stared down at the struggling figure of the girl.

'You certainly took your time,' he said bitterly. 'For a moment there I thought that I'd been shot.'

'Sorry.' A tall, thin, bearded man showed his teeth in a smile as he took a fresh grip on the girl. 'I heard the Ginzo ship land and guessed that you might be needing some help.' He nodded towards the rifle. 'Better take charge of her toy.'

'I've got it.' Handley scooped up the archaic weapon. 'Who are you?'

'My name is Winter, and I'm a doctor of sorts. The Ginzoes captured me about six months ago and I've been here ever since.' He swore as the girl bit his wrist. 'Help me with this wild cat, will you? I can't hold her.'

'Tie her up, Handley.' Ranson rubbed his bearded chin as the doctor rose to his feet. 'What's all this about?'

'The planet was colonised by a religious sect about sixty years ago. It lies well off the main space lanes and ships rarely touch down here. They have a small community back in the hills and in many ways have reverted back to a primitive life.' Winter jerked his thumb towards the ancient vessel. 'They almost worship the ship and won't let anyone stay near it. Unfortunately, the Ginzoes dumped everything of any value right beside it, and so we have to run the risk of being shot every time we want some food or supplies.'

'So that's what she meant.' Ranson nodded. 'It makes sense in a way, but I can't worry about that now. We've got to get this ship into space, and as soon as possible. How many prisoners are there?'

'About thirty. A lot of them have died, either shot or from the effects of some strange disease peculiar to the planet. The colonists could help us but they act as if we don't exist.' He stared at Ranson. 'Did you mean it? About getting the ship into space again, I mean?'

'Yes.'

'Good. I've often thought about it, but none of us are technicians, and we couldn't astrogate if we had to. Do you think we can get it working?'

'We've got to,' said Ranson grimly. He thinned his lips at the other's expression. 'The Ginzoes are getting ready to exterminate Mankind. They have a catalyst, something that can break down sodium chloride into its basic elements. You can guess what would happen if they dropped it into the oceans of the oxygen worlds.'

Winter nodded, his gaunt features grim.

'They gave us the job of warning Lasser. If we call off the war they won't use it. If we don't — ' Ranson shrugged.

'They exterminate us.' Winter nodded.

'I understand. But why did they set you down here?'

'That's our own fault. We said that we'd repair a hyper-drive unit for them; promised to do it in exchange for our lives. The Ginzoes took us literally. Now unless we can get this ship operating and the war stopped within fifty days, Mankind will be a dying memory.'

'They gave you a job,' said Winter bitterly. 'That ship hasn't moved since the day it landed sixty years ago. On top of that you've the colonists to worry about. They wouldn't let you use their precious ship if the Guardian Angel himself asked permission, and they'll shoot anyone touching it.'

'Maybe.' Ranson glanced down at the girl at his feet. 'But maybe we can do some shooting also. Can you round up all the prisoners, Winter?'

'Yes.'

'Good. Bring them here. We'll pile these crates into a barricade and work under cover. Luckily the colonists don't seem to have flare-guns and those HV rifles won't be able to penetrate the metal casings of the hyper-drive units. If the colonists get too troublesome we'll threaten to kill our hostage. If they don't seem to worry about her, then we'll try something else. Hurry now, Winter. We've got a lot to do.'

The bearded man grinned and loped away into the thickening dusk. Ranson watched him go, then, with quiet deliberation, squatted down beside the girl.

'You heard what I told him, Delila,' he said gently. 'Don't you want to help us?'

'No.'

'Be reasonable,' he urged. 'This is your struggle as much as ours. Every oxygen breathing creature is threatened by the Ginzoes and there's nothing we can do about it except to make peace with them. You have a fine world here, a nice, clean world. How would you like to see the oceans erupting great clouds of poison gas? How would you like to see the plants wither, the babies dying, every living thing coughing their lives away — and all because you refused to help?'

'I wouldn't,' she said candidly.

'Then why won't you help us?'

'It is against the Word.'

'You believe in the Word, don't you, Delila?'

'Yes.'

'Tell me, does the Word forbid lying?'

'Of course.'

'Good.' He smiled in the near-night dusk. 'When were you to be relieved?'

'At dawn.'

'What weapons and how many men?'

'Rifles and two men. I was on my own because they didn't think more prisoners had been landed. They know now and will double the guard.'

'Thank you,' he said gravely. 'Now, if I threatened to kill you, would the colonists leave us alone?'

'I don't know.'

'A pity. How many men are there in the village.'

'I — ' She stopped, her bright blue eyes shining in the ghost light from the distant stars. 'You're trying to pump me! I won't answer!'

'Remember the Word!'

'Refusing to talk isn't lying,' she said

fiercely. 'You can't make me answer.'

'No,' he admitted, and slipped the knife from her belt. 'I'd like to release you, Delila, those bonds must be uncomfortable. Will you give me your word that you won't shout, or try to escape, or to do anyone here any harm?'

'No.'

'I thought not.' Ranson sighed and rose to his feet, the knife glistening in his hand. 'Goodnight, Delila. Sleep well, and Delila — '

'Yes?'

'Thank you. There's a lot to be said for any religion that forbids lying. It makes things so much easier.'

He grinned as she tried to kick him, her long legs threshing in her bonds, then became serious as he stared into the night. One day gone and nothing done. Forty-nine left and half the galaxy to be saved.

Grimly he sat down and waited for the coming of dawn.

9

The Word

Dawn came with a flood of pink and orange, staining the clear blue of the cloudless sky and tinging the heavens with golden glory. With the dawn came the dumped prisoners, thin, hungry looking, almost animal in their hate of the colonists who had refused to help them. They grabbed thermocans, thrusting in the cone-shaped tops and impatiently waiting for the built-in chemical units to heat the vitaminised soup. With the dawn came also the capture of two more hostages and two of the long barrelled high velocity rifles.

Ranson almost laughed at the simplicity of the capture.

The guards had entered the small clump of trees, calling for the girl to show herself. They had called, groaned, and slumped unconscious as Handley and the young commander had wielded branches

139

to good effect. Now they rested beside the girl, their eyes wild with fury as they saw the desecration of their shrine, and two more rifles had been added to the arsenal of the prisoners.

Impatiently Ranson set the dumped prisoners to work.

They heaved the thick casing of the ruined hyper-drive units into a rough circle, filling in the gaps with boxes and bales of supplies, broken components, anything solid that would stop the tiny missiles of the HV rifles. Not until the barrier was completed did Ranson let them relax, and then he detailed guards to watch the surrounding area while others broke out food and drink.

Over a steaming thermocan of ener-gised soup he gave terse instructions.

'Winter, you've been here long enough to know most of these people. I want you to act as medical officer and nominal head. Handley, you and I will inspect the ship and do what we can to get it into space. Any help we need we'll get from the others.' He gulped at the soup and grimaced as he wiped the back of his hand across his bearded lips. 'The first thing I want is a bath and a shave. Any razors among your crowd, Winter?'

'A couple. We haven't bothered to use them, though. I told you of the strange disease, which attacked some of us after landing here. Well, I had the idea that it could be caused by an aerobic bacteria. Shaving may be a good idea, but it damages the skin and permits infection to start.' The doctor shrugged. 'I'm perfectly willing to admit that I'm only guessing, but personally, I'll put up with the beard while I'm here. Looking clean can wait.'

'Yes,' said Ranson grimly. 'I see what you mean.' He stared at the towering bulk of the ancient space ship. 'Get what tools you think we'll need, Handley. Winter, you sort out these supplies and keep an eye on things in general. I don't have to tell you what to do, but remember, time is running out and we want no laying down on the job.'

He rose, tossing aside the empty thermocan, and the engineer grunted as he lifted a tool kit and followed the young commander.

The ship was a wreck.

Ranson stared at it, his nostrils wrinkling as he smelt the musty air, and his eyes narrowed as he examined the control room and essential components. The general layout of the controls was similar to those on more modern vessels, and he threw several switches, watching the weak flicker of gauges and dials. Handley stamped into the room, his broad face glistening with sweat and streaked with dirt and oil.

'What's the verdict, Carl?'

'Not good. This vessel has lain unused for too long. It will take a lot of work to get it space-worthy again. How is the hyper-drive unit?'

Handley shrugged.

'The coolant has evaporated, of course, and the coils are a little out of adjustment. It isn't ruined though, and I may be able to get it working.' He glanced at the controls. 'How is the pile?'

'Low. We'll have to restock it with fissionable elements. Then we must check the wiring and lights. The generator wants attention and naturally the air system is all to hell.' Ranson bit his lip as he looked at the control panel. 'Luckily there seems to be enough fuel for take-off, but the entire ship needs a thorough overhaul. Even with a complete workshop and skilled men it would take weeks — and we haven't got that much time.'

'Does the radio work?'

'No. Even if it did, I doubt whether it could reach very far. Anyway, this is a normal radio, not a faster than light hyper-beam set, and it would take years for any message from here to reach Earth.' He frowned at the engineer.

'We'll have to get this crate into space, Handley. There is nothing else we can do.'

'Then let's get on with it.' The big man wiped his face and stared at the dirt streaking the back of his hand.

'How do we operate, Carl?'

'Strip the pile and generator. We must have lights and power. Then, while we are rebuilding the atomic pile you check the hyper-drive unit, that is the most important of all. Then, if we can, we'll replace all essential wiring and get the radio working.' Ranson shrugged as he stared around the control room. 'It's lucky that they don't have rats on this planet. Those fools of colonists left the air lock open, and if this had been Earth there wouldn't have been a scrap of insulation left on a single wire.' He grinned at the engineer. 'Cheer up, Handley! It could be worse.'

'Yeah?' The big man grunted as he reached for his tools. 'That's what you think!'

Morosely he stamped away and the young commander heard his soft cursing as he stooped over the time-settled bulk of the generator and pile.

Winter sat on the soft grass, his back against a thick metal casing, and the long barrelled HV rifle resting across his knees. The doctor seemed asleep, but his eyes gleamed from time to time and his hands never strayed from the smooth butt of the weapon. He looked up as Ranson left the ship. 'When do we leave?'

'Maybe never.' Carl reached for one of the cone-shaped thermocans. 'Winter. You know what men we can rely on. Are there any technicians? Radio men, atom jacks, generator engineers?'

'There's a radio man, and I think that a couple of others served as rocket riders on a cargo ship once. Shall I get them?'

'Later.' Ranson thrust in the top of the thermocan and held it between his palms, swirling it a little as he waited for the built-in chemical unit to heat the energised soup. 'We've a lot of work to do on the ship before it will lift, Winter. Handley thinks that he can repair the hyperdrive, but we need help.'

'You've got it,' said the doctor promptly. Ranson shook his head.

'We need something more than just a few pairs of willing hands. We need those, too, of course, but it really boils down to the fact that only Handley, myself, and the radio man you mentioned are going to be of much real use.'

'I see.'

'There's one way in which you could help, Winter.'

Ranson sniffed at the steaming thermocan and took a deep swallow of the hot soup. 'You could fix us something so that we could do without sleep. Something like neo-benzedrine or ultra caffeine. Can you do that?'

'I doubt it,' Winter frowned. 'They didn't leave me my medical kit when they dumped me here, and drugs like that are hard to make. Must you have them?'

'Yes.' Ranson tilted the thermocan and tossed the empty metal container aside. 'We have just over forty days for what we have to do. That isn't long enough, Winter. The only way out is for us to do without sleep for a while. That way we can work twenty-four hours a day instead of sixteen. How about the ship supplies? Would they be any use after all this time?'

'If the drugs were packed in vacuum containers, they would be.' Winter surged to his feet. 'Let's have a look at them.'

'Wait.' Ranson didn't move towards the ship. 'I've already looked, the medical kit has gone.'

'Then — '

'The colonists must have taken it from the vessel when they landed. It would be a natural thing to do.'

'Then they are gone.' Winter bit his lips with annoyance. 'We can't get them now, and anyway, they probably used them or threw them away.'

'Perhaps not.' Ranson glanced to where the three hostages rested against the hull of the old ship their arms and legs tied with strips of cloth. 'They almost worship this vessel, and maybe, just maybe, they may have a local shrine. In any case, they wouldn't have had any need for the anti-sleep pills, and, if they looked after the medical kit with half the care they looked after the ship, they should still have them.'

'Yes, Ranson, but they would have them in their village. We can't get them. We'd be shot on sight.'

'We would,' agreed the young commander. 'But maybe they would think twice about shooting one of their own kind.' He glanced towards the prisoners, and Winter nodded with understanding.

'Would they do it,'

'I don't know,' said Ranson grimly. 'But we can try.' He stepped towards the glaring eyes of the bound men.

'Listen,' he said urgently. 'I want to know one thing. At your village do you have a small metal box, a medical kit, which was taken from the ship when your people first landed here?'

No answer. They lay and glared at him, two men and a girl, and Ranson sighed as he recognised the hate in their eyes.

'I hate to do this,' he said quietly, and metal gleamed in his hand as he drew the girl's knife from his belt. 'But unless you answer my questions I am going to operate on the girl. Now. Do you have such an object in your village?'

Silence.

'I mean what I say.' Deliberately the young man lowered the shining blade until the needlepoint rested on the girl's soft throat. 'Unless you answer me I shall drive this knife into her gullet.' He pressed on the blade and a point of bright red blood marred the smooth perfection of her skin. 'Does your Word permit you to watch the killing of an innocent girl?'

'You will burn for this!' One of the men twisted in his bonds and sweat glistened on his bearded face.

'Maybe, but the life of this girl is in your hands. Answer my questions or she

148

dies!' Again Ranson pressed on the blade and a moan echoed from between the girl's lips.

'Yes. Damn you, yes! Now leave her alone.'

'So you do have the medical kit.' Ranson smiled as he stared at the bearded man. 'Now, listen to me. I'm not going to waste time in arguing with you. What I do I do for the sake of every living thing on every oxygen world in the galaxy. I can't afford to be gentle with ignorance, and so I tell you this. Unless that metal box is brought here. Unless we are left alone to work and our orders obeyed — I shall destroy your village!'

'You — '

'I shall raise the ship from the ground and I shall smash it to atoms in the heart of your settlement. I swear this. I swear it by the Word.' He stared into the hate-filled eyes of the bearded man. 'Now, I am going to free your bonds. You will return to your village and bring me the metal box. You will tell your Elders that we are to be left alone. If you do not obey me then I will kill the girl and the other man. I shall lift the ancient vessel and I will destroy it and destroy your village as well. I mean this.'

The man swallowed, his muscles tensing as he fought his bonds. 'Damn you! What devil sent you here to torment us?'

'A devil called necessity,' said Ranson quietly. 'Now. Do you swear to do as I ask?'

'I swear.'

'Do you swear by the Word?' Ranson lifted the knife, the glittering point hovering an inch above the throat of the helpless girl.

'I swear by the Word,' gasped the man, and sagged as if at a tremendous revulsion of feeling. Ranson nodded and cut his bonds.

'Go in peace,' he said gently. 'Hurry back with the box and fear nothing. I, too, have sworn by the Word.' He stepped back and watched the man bite his lips against the pain of returning circulation, then, as his limbs eased, the native ran through the crowd, jumped the barricade, and ran with a long, loping stride towards the horizon.

Ranson sighed and turned away, not liking what he saw in the girl's contemptuous eyes. Winter joined him, and the doctor's gaunt features were thoughtful as he stared after the running man.

'Would you have killed her, Ranson?'

'What?' Ranson shrugged. 'I don't know. We are playing for too high a stake for the life of any one person to matter, Winter. Unless we can stop this war all of us, men, women, children, even the animals and insects will die. None of us can have any regard for anything but saving our race. The danger is too great.'

'But would you have killed her?'

'No.'

'I thought not.' Winter sighed with relief. 'For a moment you had me worried back there. I almost interfered.'

'If you had done I would have killed you,' said Ranson coldly. 'I wouldn't have harmed the girl because she wasn't a free agent, but you would have been different.' He stared at the gaunt-faced man. 'I'm, not joking about this thing, Winter. You didn't see what I saw. You weren't facing the Ginzoes and you didn't hear the babblings of a madman. I did. I know that the Ginzoes mean exactly what they say, and I know that unless we can make Lasser call off this war, we are as good as dead. Remember that, Winter. Remember it if you are tempted to interfere on some other occasion.'

'I'll remember.' Winter shivered a little as he glanced at the grim features of the young man. Ranson smiled.

'That man will return with the medical kit and he will tell his Elders what I threatened. They will leave us alone now. They hold their Word to be sacred and they will not break it, not even to save their precious ship.' He sighed a little as he watched the thin figures of the dumped men and women as they struggled with the heaps of supplies. 'This is a nice planet, Winter, and there is a lot to be said for a religion which eliminates lying and deceit. Almost I wish — ' His voice trailed into silence and almost unconsciously he turned his head and glanced to where Delila rested against the hard metal of the hull.

'You wish what, Ranson?'

'Nothing. Release those two when the messenger returns. Make them give you their word not to escape, and set them to work, all three of them. We can use every pair of hands now.'

'I understand,' said Winter softly. 'She is very attractive.'

'You're a fool,' snapped Ranson, and abruptly turned and headed towards the ship.

Winter shrugged.

10

Takeoff

The ship hummed with energy and noise. Lights blazed from the fluorescents and the smell of hot oil and burned metal eddied from the engine room and stung the nostrils of sweating workers. Ranson slumped into the pilot's chair and threw several toggles, reading the flickering dials with burning eyes.

'Any good?' Handley rested his huge frame against the bulkhead and blinked at the young commander.

'Better. The pile is 'hot' and we've plenty of energy from the generator. The controls have been rewired and the lights are working again.' He sniffed at the stale air. 'I wish that we could get the air system in some sort of working order.'

'It's taken us thirty days to strip and restock the pile, overhaul the generator and rewire the circuits.' Handley rubbed at his sore eyes. 'It would take as long again to get the air and reclamation systems working.' He yawned again. 'How is the radio?'

'Working.' Ranson fumbled in his pocket and took out a phial of blue tablets. He shook one on to his palm and put it in his mouth, swallowing and grimacing at the taste.

'You'd better go easy on those things,' warned the big man. 'Winter says that the neo-benzedrine may have deteriorated after so long.'

'It has,' said Ranson grimly. 'It's unpredictable, tastes like hell, and is probably poisoning us — but what can we do about it? To get this wreck into some sort of condition we've got to work on it. We just can't afford to sleep, we haven't that much time.' Wearily he turned the control panel and began to check the registering instruments,

'Pile: sixty percent optimum. Lights: fifty percent. Generator: fifty-five percent. Fuel: fifteen percent of capacity.' He looked towards the engineer. 'How are the tubes, Handley?'

'As well as can be expected after sixty

years without attention.' The big man sagged against the bulkhead. 'I haven't dismantled them, couldn't do it without cranes and jacks but they seem in good condition.'

Ranson nodded and stared again at the flickering dials.

'Ion discharge. Not operating. Air system. Not operating. Visi-screens.' He threw a switch and stared at the murky plastic. 'About thirty percent light transmission. Radio. Good. Intercom. Good enough.' He yawned and returned the switches to neutral. 'That's about it, Handley. As soon as we load up with water and compressed air we'll be off.'

'Then the real trouble starts,' said the engineer gloomily. 'We still don't know if the hyper-drive unit is working. I can't test it until we're in flight.'

'Have you checked it?'

'Yes. It should work, but you know how those things are. Unless they're in perfect synchronisation the coils won't establish the field. I can tune them by hand — unless the ultrasonic kills me first, but it isn't easy.'

'I know it.' Ranson rose from his chair and stumbled as he crossed the control room. 'Tell your gang to clear up and batten down. I'll get Winter to supervise the water detail, and you can get some men filling the oxygen tanks with compressed air. It won't be much good, but it'll be better than nothing. How are we for food?'

'Enough. There's a couple of cases of thermocans not touched yet.'

'Right.' Ranson stumbled again, and paused, rubbing his eyes and shaking his head. 'I'm about all in.'

'Why don't you get some sleep, Carl?' Handley straightened and steadied the young commander with one big hand. 'The way you are you're liable to make mistakes, and you don't make mistakes in space — not twice you don't.'

'I'll sleep later, when we are on our way, but until then sleep must wait.' He grunted as he staggered against the metal of a stanchion. 'Help me outside. I'll dip my head in water and the fresh air will jerk me awake.'

Handley nodded and helped the young

man out of the ship into the crisp morning air.

Winter joined them as they leaned against the scarred hull of the ancient vessel. The gaunt doctor seemed worried and he plucked at his beard, his sunken eyes thoughtful, as he stared at the group of men and women gathered around the sorted supplies.

'I've heard that the air system doesn't work,' he said abruptly. 'Is that correct?'

'Yes.'

'Then how are you going to manage? Thirty people use quite a lot of oxygen and even with tanks of compressed air we aren't going to get very far.'

'I know that.' Ranson yawned, then breathed deeply of the chill air. A woman passed him, a tall, well-made girl, and he stopped, her, pointing to the container of water she carried.

'Let me have that, will you?'

'Can I stop you?' Delila stared coldly at the young man. 'I'd like to throw it over you, but if I did you'd probably cut my throat.'

'Try me.' He smiled at her, feeling

strangely glad that she hadn't left them after she had been freed. 'Go on,' he urged. 'I mean it.'

For a moment she stared at him, then, a tight smile on her full lips, lifted the container. 'You asked for it, mister!' Deliberately she threw the water directly into his face.

Ranson coughed, spluttered, then, shivering from the impact of the icy water, grinned.

'Thank you, Delila.' He glanced at Winter, and the doctor answered his unspoken question.

'All three of them decided to stay and help. I gave them their choice after the first ten days, when we were certain that the colonists wouldn't attack, but they didn't seem to want to leave.'

'Why not?'

'I wanted to stay,' said Delila coldly. 'I wanted to find out what it was that made a man forget himself and threaten a woman. The men stayed to protect me.'

'Do you need protection?'

'I don't know.' Delila stared at the young man. 'Do I?'

Ranson shrugged. 'Not from me, you don't.' He rubbed his tired eyes and glanced at the engineer, 'Could you show her where to put the water, Handley?'

'Yeah. You going to start loading the ship now?'

'Why not? The quicker we get into space the better.'

The young commander looked at the tall girl. 'Do as he tells you, Delila. Make certain that every drop of water going into the tanks has been boiled and filtered. We don't want it going bad on us after we start.'

'You taking me with you?'

'What?'

'You heard me,' she said coldly. 'I'm asking if I'm going with you.'

'Do you want to come?'

'Would I ask if I didn't?'

'But — ' Ranson paused. 'Look, you load the water and we'll see what can be done later. If you want to come I'll try to make a place for you. Good enough?'

'Yes.' Suddenly she smiled and Ranson saw what the doctor had meant when he had said that she was very attractive.

160

'Thanks, mister. I'd like to go with you. I've been talking to the others and there seems to be a lot going on that I didn't know about.'

'Right. You get to work now.' Ranson stared after her, noting the lithe ease of her carriage and the supple perfection of her figure. He sighed, and Winter stirred restlessly at his side.

'Did you mean that?'

'About taking her with us? Of course not.'

'Then why tell her you would?'

'Because I'm too tired to argue, that's why, Winter. What use would I have for a girl from a backwoods planet? Damn it, man! This isn't a holiday we're going on. We've got to stop a war.'

'I'm glad that you remember it,' said the gaunt man drily. 'Now, about the air. Do you think we can compress enough to last us all?'

'No.'

'Then — '

'Isn't it obvious, Winter?' Ranson forced his heavy lids to remain open. 'We can't all go. There's no point in it anyway.

I'm taking Handley, the radio operator, you, and one other man to help out in the engine room. Five of us. We can last on the compressed air and we can operate the ship. The rest must stay here.'

'They won't like it, Ranson.'

'Then they can lump it! Damn it all, Winter, I can't worry about what a handful of people want. We can always send for them later. Now we have a job to do and they must take second place.' He paused, his eyes narrowing, and stared out over the surrounding plain.

'What is it?' Winter rose to his full height and squinted across the barrier.

'People. Lots of people.' The young commander stared at the gaunt doctor. 'The colonists! They are heading this way.'

'I wonder — ' Winter broke off as the faint sound of distant singing echoed from the advancing villagers 'Delila! What is happening?'

'I don't know.' She halted next to where they stood, the water slopping from her container and running over her booted feet. 'They gave their Word. I — '

'Delila!' One of the captured guards sprang towards her. 'Away! Away before the fires of vengeance burst on these devils! The Elders are coming, and they will cleanse this spot with fire and sword. Away!'

'Hold it!' Ranson stepped forward. 'They swore by the Word not to molest us. Why are they here?'

'Today is the Day of Landing!' Fanatical zealotry burned in the guard's eyes. 'On this day we give thanks to our forefathers and pay homage to the Ship. On this day our ancestors landed here, fleeing from hate and persecution. They found this fair world and settled here to bring the Word and the true way of life. On this day we are not bound by any promise. Beware spawn of Hell! The Elders come!'

He glared at the tall girl.

'Well, Delila? Do you obey or will you remain with these beasts to be eliminated?'

'She's staying here,' snapped Ranson curtly. 'And so are you. Handley!'

'Yes?'

'Call a couple of men and bring me a rifle.'

'Trouble?'

'Maybe. Hurry, will you.' Ranson stared at the bearded man. 'We'll see about vengeance. Didn't anyone ever tell you that vengeance has a double edge? We can kill, too, you know, and will unless we are left alone.'

The man glared, baring his teeth in an animal-snarl, then, with amazing speed, he twisted, turned, knocked down a woman and was racing towards the barricade.

'Handley!' Ranson glanced around for the big man. 'Where's that gun?'

'Here.' The engineer thrust the long barrelled weapon into Ranson's hands. 'What's the matter?'

'War.' Ranson lifted the gun and squinted along the sights. He thinned his lips, aiming at the dwindling figure of the running man, and slowly, very slowly, his finger squeezed the trigger.

'Don't!' A hand thrust up the barrel and the tiny missile whined towards the morning sky. 'How can you kill him?'

'How?' Ranson glared at the girl and something in his eyes made her whiten and step back. 'By putting a bullet in his body, of course. How else? Damn you, girl. Why did you ruin my chance?'

'He was my friend,' she whispered. 'I couldn't see him shot down like a dog.'

'Now he will bring the colonists down on us. He knows our exact strength and the total resources of the men here. I could have bluffed them with the turret gun if you hadn't interfered. Now they will know that it can't be fired, that the electrodes and firing chamber are corroded and useless. They will attack. They have fifty guns to our three. Food, water, all the time in the galaxy. We have nothing.'

'I'm sorry,' she whispered, 'but he has been my friend.'

'And so we all die.' Bitterly Ranson threw the rifle towards a staring man. 'Take your place at the barricade. Handley!'

'Yes?'

'Tie up that other hostage.'

'Too late,' said the big man grimly. 'He

tried to grab a rifle and got knifed.'

'Good.' Ranson flinched as something exploded high on the hull of the ancient vessel. 'They're firing at us. Take cover, everyone. Conserve your shots.'

'What shall we do, Ranson?' Winter stared at the young commander, his gaunt face worried beneath its tangle of beard. 'We can't hold them off for long. We've only three rifles with limited ammunition. Most of the food is in the ship and all the water we have is in the tanks.'

'That's not much, either.' Handley scowled towards the firing colonists. 'We only had time to sterilize a few pints.' He looked at Ranson. 'Shall we shelter within the ship?'

'No. Once they get close they can do too much damage.' Ranson looked at the group of ragged men and pale-faced women. He swallowed, then, with almost savage abruptness, rapped quick orders.

'Handley! Get that radio operator and the man to help you in the engine room. Take them aboard, Winter. You come with me.' He hesitated, looking at the girl.

'They won't harm you, Delila. Just stay

under cover and you'll be all right.'

'What are you going to do, Ranson?' Winter stared accusingly at the young man. Ranson shrugged.

'The only thing we can do. We're taking off.'

'All of us?'

'No.'

'You intend to leave these people here?' The gaunt doctor shook his head. 'No, Ranson. You can't do it. They won't have a chance against the colonists, and you know it. If you leave them behind you, you are as good as murdering them.'

'Damn you, Winter! Do you have to say that?' The young commander clenched his hands until the knuckles showed white beneath the skin. 'What else can we do? The ship hasn't any water and we've a long way to go. Do you want me to take these people with us? Do you want to watch them die of thirst? No, Winter. I know what I'm doing. After we have gone they can surrender to the colonists, but they can't come with us, and that's final!'

'If they don't go, then I stay here.'

'You're going to do as you are told,

Winter. Too much depends on us for you to get squeamish now. You're coming. Now. Get into the ship!'

'No.'

'I warn you, man. Don't cross me. I've stood all I'm capable of taking. Get into that ship!'

'No.' Winter shook his head. 'You aren't responsible for what you say, Ranson. I warned you about that neo-benzedrine. You're poisoned, half-dead from want of rest. If you weren't you wouldn't think of abandoning these people.'

'You're wrong, Winter. What are the lives of thirty people against the lives of the billions inhabiting the oxygen worlds? They don't matter. We don't matter. I don't matter. Nothing matters except getting that warning through to Lasser on Earth. We are the only ones who can do it. Therefore we go. Now!'

'No. I — ' Winter broke off, a startled expression on his bearded features, then slumped forward, a trickle of blood running from beneath his hair.

'I believe you,' said Delila simply. 'Let me help you get him on the ship.'

Ranson nodded, feeling strangely light-headed, and together they carried the limp figure of the doctor towards the open airlock. Handley met them halfway, and the big man grunted as he threw the gaunt man over one shoulder.

'Better hurry, Carl. They're getting suspicious.'

Ranson nodded and ran ahead towards the open airlock. He didn't look behind. He didn't think of anything except the pressing need of getting into space and heading towards Earth. Numbly he slipped into the pilot's chair and reached for the ranked controls. The visi-screen flashed to life, the fluorescents, and as he switched on the intercom a red lamp flashed on the panel.

'Control here. All aboard?'

'All aboard, Carl.' Handley's voice echoed thinly from the speaker. 'Shall I seal her up?'

'Yes. Close ports. Stand by for priming.'

Red lamps flashed as the external locks closed, and others glowed as the young commander fed fuel to the gaping venturis. A mutter swelled from the base of the vessel. A deep-throated, roaring sound, and fire sprayed from the base of the ancient ship, searing the ground and turning the grass black and ugly.

Outside the ship men cursed and swore, shaking their arms and firing at the scarred hull. Ranson watched them in the dull visi-screen, then, when they had retreated to a safe distance, reached for the controls.

'Stand by for take-off. Minus five! Four! Three! Two! One! Zero!'

A lever moved softly in its groove and the deep-throated thunder of the idling venturis grew to a snarling roar. Sound blasted from the base of the vessel. A shrilling, screaming, whistling roar of unleashed energy. Fire spouted from the rocket tubes, and the grass blackened and the loam fused to smoking ash beneath the incredible heat of the exhaust.

Slowly the ship began to rise.

It rose as if reluctant to leave the place where it had rested for more than sixty years. It lifted its massed tons of weight into the clear air and it screamed its giant's protest as it rose on wings of flame. Slowly, then faster, then faster still as if, once started, it was in a hurry to be gone. Faster, faster, until it climbed towards the cold stars and the limitless wastes of space.

Inside the control room Ranson groaned as the crushing weight of acceleration pressure piled invisible tons of lead on to his shrinking flesh. Grimly he kept the firing lever hard down, knowing that the shortage of fuel prevented the slower, but more wasteful, take-off.

Numbly he stared at the dull surface of the visi-screen, watching the blue of the sky give way to black, to star-shot ebon, to the empty coldness of outer space. Blood oozed from his bitten lips as he fought against blacking out. He had to remain conscious! This old wreck had no automatic cut-outs, and if he lost his battle they would drive on and on, streaking across the void until their fuel gave out and then they would drift forever, lifeless, helpless, a dead ship with a dead crew.

Still the acceleration pressure increased,

thrusting him deep into the padding of the pilot's chair and seeming to crush his chest and drive his head down between his shoulders.

On the panel the flickering needles of the gauges danced and swung across the dials as the temperature of the rocket tubes rose and the fuel in the tanks lowered.

Ranson glared at them, forcing his eyes, weighted by lack of sleep and the thrust of acceleration, to remain open as he studied the instruments. They weren't rising fast enough. The rate of ascent was using too much fuel and unless they reached escape velocity soon they would have none for spatial manoeuvring.

Deliberately he reached for the firing lever.

Weight piled on his protesting body. Terrible weight, seeming to strip the very flesh from his bones and to churn his internal organs to a compressed pulp. Before his eyes the instrument panel seemed to recede into a tunnel of ebon night, and dimly, as if from a tremendous distance, he heard a woman scream.

Then he was thrusting at the levers, cutting their acceleration, quenching the thrusting fire stabbing from the venturis. Weight vanished as the ship fell into free fall, and he gulped, swaying in the padded chair.

They were in space!

He sighed, and, with a tremendous effort, forced himself to plot their course and to check the controls. He swayed as he rose from the chair, and he grabbed at the back of the seat, cursing himself for forgetting the metal-soled shoes necessary in free fall. He cursed, then grinned, feeling the rush of blood through his brain and the well-remembered euphoria experienced in the transition period as his body adjusted itself to the lack of gravity,

Then everything seemed to dissolve and swirl in a confused pattern of instruments and control levers, of lights and visi-screen, of pilot's chair and stanchions, and he was falling — falling — falling.

Falling into the black night of utter exhaustion.

11

Breakthrough

He was in Hell. It was raining and a damned soul was screaming in his ear. Ranson groaned; striking out with his arms, and trying to shield his face from the dripping rain. He writhed, lifting his hands to his ears, gritting his teeth against the screams. Hands caught him and abruptly he was fully awake.

Delila smiled down at him.

He stared at her with startled disbelief, then winced as a shrilling hum droned through the ship.

'How did you get here?'

'Walked on, of course.' She smiled at his blank expression. 'I followed you and your engineer. Handley must have thought you knew about it.' She frowned at bitter memory. 'I was sorry to leave my people and for a moment I thought that I would die. Are takeoffs always like that?'

'Not always.' Ranson rolled from the narrow bunk and wiped his wet face. 'What were you trying to do? Drown me?'

'No. Winter was worried about you. You have been asleep for two days now.'

'Two days.' Ranson surged to his feet. 'Why didn't you wake me sooner?' He licked parched lips and reached for the water with which she had bathed his face. 'Where's Handley?' He winced as the droning shrill echoed throughout the ship. 'Don't bother to answer that. I can guess what he's doing.' Greedily he gulped the water and stood, his metallic boots clinging to the deck plates, while he waited for his head to clear from the lingering traces of sleep. He felt hungry, and, due to the after effects of the anti-sleep drugs, a little light headed.

'I'm going to the engine room,' he said. 'Bring me some food, will you, Delila? A couple of thermocans will do.' He smiled at her and moved away.

Handley grunted as he entered the machine-cluttered engine room. The engineer was stripped to the waist, his huge torso glistening with sweat and stained with dirt and oil. He crouched over the squat bulk of the hyper-drive and his big, strangely delicate hands, rested on the knurled knobs of vernier controls.

'Thank God you're awake, Carl.' The big man straightened and kicked at the hyper-drive unit. 'This damn thing's got me beat. Every time I try to adjust it Winter alters the power flow. We just can't get started.'

'Have you plotted our course?' Ranson smiled at the girl as she entered the room, carrying several opened thermocans. Handley shook his head.

'No. I don't know much about astrogation. I showed him what switches to throw and then came down here. It's no good though, Carl. The Doc doesn't know the first thing about energy flow, and I can't tune this thing without expert help.'

'What about the others?'

'The radio operator and the other man?'

'Yes.'

'I couldn't find them, Carl. Anyway, they would only have been in the way.

Used water and eaten food we couldn't spare. We can do without them.'

'It seems as if we'll have to,' said Ranson drily. 'One day, Handley, you'll learn to obey orders.' He shrugged and took a long drink of energized soup. 'Let's get up to the control room. I want to find out just where we are.'

In the control room Winter sat, staring blankly at the ranked instruments, his sunken eyes worried and haggard. He smiled as he saw Ranson and slipped from the chair.

'Glad you're awake, Ranson. You had me worried. I warned you about those drugs, remember? You took an awful chance.'

'Never mind that now.' Ranson slipped into the control chair and reached for the instruments. 'We must find out just where we are, align the ship, and start the hyper-drive.' He frowned at the glittering array of stars. 'This looks like the Altair sector. That blue-white star and that giant red — ' His voice trailed into silence as he connected the visi-screen to the computer. The surrounding star fields were analyzed and matched to the records in the computer. Within seconds the results showed in the display window. Ranson grunted in satisfaction. 'We're about sixty light years from Earth, say three days hyper-drive travel.' He looked at the big man. 'What are you waiting for, Handley? Let's get started.'

'Aren't you going to align the ship?'

'I can do that while you're getting the unit ready. When we start I don't want to have to stop for anything. We haven't the time for visiting.'

Tensely the young commander stooped over the controls.

'How do you align the ship?' Winter frowned as he looked at the visi-screen. 'They all look alike to me.'

'We find out where we are from the computer. Then we pick a target star and align the ship directly towards it. I'll start the rocket drive in a moment to give us forward momentum. Once the ship is aimed straight we cut in the hyper-drive and enter hyperspace. You know, of course, that in hyperspace our rate of travel in relation to the normal universe is in a ratio of one hour to one light year?'

'I know that.'

'So all we have to do is to aim the ship right, enter hyperspace, and emerge after a predicted number of hours. That is the theory. If nothing goes wrong we should emerge within a hundred million miles of Sol.'

'Can anything go wrong?'

'We could make a mistake and emerge within a planet or within the target star. We could aim wrong and emerge off-course. The hyper-drive unit could break down and leave us stranded between worlds, light years from any possible assistance. The unit could be faulty and kill us all with ultrasonic.' Ranson shrugged and weight returned with the thunder of rockets as he carefully adjusted the flight path of the space ship.

'Aside from all that we've nothing to worry about.' He leaned forward and threw the toggle of the intercom. 'Ready, Handley?'

'Ready!'

'Stand by for power.' A thin shrilling

echoed through the vessel, the speeded humming of the generator feeding power to the ranked accumulators supplying the hyper-drive coils. The lights dimmed, then flared, then steadied to their normal glow. Ranson licked his lips, his hand resting on a small lever.

'Watch it, Handley. I'm cutting in the hyper-drive.'

'Let her go!'

Ranson grinned and pressed down on the lever.

Strain gripped them. A peculiar, mind twisting, body-wrenching sensation of warped atoms and distorted molecules. For a moment a peculiar grey mist seemed to swirl throughout the vessel, then —

Delila screamed and pressed her hands against her ears. Winter groaned, blood rilling from his nose and mouth. Ranson swore, jerked, swore again as his hands danced over the controls.

'Handley! Kill that ultrasonic!'

'I'm trying!' The big engineer's voice sounded thin with agony. 'Feed me power.'

The lights died to a dull red glow. The visi-screen went dark and the shrill, almost inaudible whining from the hyper-drive unit faded from the dangerous regions of ultrasonic vibration. Again the grey mist swirled around them and again it seemed as if a giant, invisible hand had seized the vessel and was slowly twisting it inside out.

Again the stabbing agony, and Ranson snarled with soundless rage as his hands darted over the unfamiliar controls, keeping the flow of power to the hyper-drive unit faded from the dangerous regions of ultrasonic vibration. Again the grey mist swirled around them and again the sensation of strain gripped the ship and everything within its hull. This time it didn't fade, it increased, grew, and abruptly with a stomach twisting sense of utter nausea, it had passed.

They were through.

Ranson sagged in his chair, wiping the blood from his bitten lips, and his hands trembled as he adjusted the controls. On the dull surface of the visi-screen a thick grey mist swirled with a peculiar, almost alien life and he stared at it with heavy eyes.

'What happened?' Winter dabbed at his ears and nose. 'Did anything break?'

'Not quite. The unit wasn't adjusted correctly and we had a lot of ultrasonic vibration. If it hadn't been for Handley we could never have established the field. As an engineer he can't be beaten, there aren't more than a dozen men capable of tuning a hyper-drive unit while in flight.'

'Are we all right now?'

'It depends on what you mean by 'all right'. If you mean that the hyper-drive is working you could be right — after a fashion. Don't forget that this ship was left for more than sixty years without any attention or maintenance. We've worked on it for thirty days without proper equipment and sticking to the essentials. The ship is in space, it is in hyperspace, but personally, I'd rather not be on it at all.'

'As bad as that?'

'Just that.' Ranson stared at the gaunt doctor, his grey eyes serious, then smiled at the girl. 'Well, Delila. How do you like your first experience of space flight?'

'I don't,' she said promptly, and Ranson smiled.

'It isn't always as bad as this. On the big passenger transports you hardly notice the breakthrough, and they use plenty of fuel for an easy takeoff. You've had the worst takeoff and breakthrough possible.'

'Breakthrough?'

'Yes. Breaking through from normal to hyperspace. Don't you know about that?'

'No. Will you explain it to me?'

'Maybe later, or perhaps the Doc would like to fill in the gaps for you.' Ranson rose to his feet. 'Funny thing about hyperspace though, there is no free fall. It always feels as though the rockets are operating.'

'Why is that?' Winter stared at the young commander as he asked the question. Ranson shrugged.

'If I could answer that one I'd be famous. The only thing any one really knows about hyperspace is that we appear able to travel in it. Just where or what it is we can only guess.'

He stared at the instrument panel and adjusted a vernier control. 'I'm going to see if everything is all right. Perhaps you'd like to get some food and water, Delila. I feel hungry after that long sleep.'

'Can I come?' Winter stepped forward.

'Why not,' she said absently, and the gaunt doctor grinned beneath his beard.

Together they left the control room.

In the engine room Handley crouched over the humming bulk of the hyper-drive and listened with intense concentration to the whispering drone of semi-inaudible sound.

'Will it hold out?' Ranson rested his ear against the casing and gritted his teeth at the bone-jarring vibration. The engineer grunted and slowly rose, wiping his hands on the legs of his slacks.

'I doubt it. The whole thing is out of tune. I was lucky to hit the right combination so as to create the field.'

'I noticed that. Drained all the power, too. How is the leakage?'

'Bad. I'm using half the output of the generator to keep the field stable. If it gets any worse the field will collapse and we'll emerge somewhere between the stars.' He shuddered. 'You know what that means.'

'I know.' Ranson bared his teeth in a tiger-snarl as he stared at the obsolete unit. 'Damn the Ginzoes! Why couldn't they have given us a decent ship to carry their message? Why, for that matter, couldn't they have radioed it through themselves?'

'Maybe they're bluffing us?'

'I doubt it. They could have fixed the demonstration, it wouldn't have been hard to arrange a tank of chlorine beneath that bowl of water, but somehow I think that they are sincere. Anyway, they couldn't have arranged Warren. That man was insane with power-lust.'

'Yes,' said the engineer, and slowly closed his big fists. 'I was a fool. He died too easily.'

'He died,' said Ranson curtly. 'How, doesn't matter. It's what he left behind him that we've got to worry about.' Irritably he began pacing the deck plates of the engine room. 'They gave us fifty days. We wasted two after landing. Then thirty getting the ship into some sort of shape. I've been asleep for another two. Thirty-four days gone. Sixteen days to get to Earth, contact Lasser, and make him end the war. Sixteen days, and it will take at least three at the fastest rate of travel known to get to Earth!'

'If we are lucky.' Handley scowled at the hyper-drive.

'If this thing lasts for three days I'll grow wings. It's vibrating, Carl. Building up resonance. If for no other reason, we'll have to emerge and allow the ultrasonic to damp out.'

'We daren't emerge. If we do we may land smack in the middle of a planet.' Ranson glared at the whispering machine. 'Even if we miss immediate destruction we could never re-establish the field. That wreck of a generator just can't deliver power fast enough. It was only because we'd charged the accumulators that we managed to swing the balance last time. No, Handley. I don't care if we bleed at every joint. We've got to keep going!'

Handley shrugged, started to speak, then fell silent as the doctor and the girl entered the room. Winter had a worried gleam in his eyes, and both of them carried thermocans.

'Thanks.' Ranson took a couple of the cans from Delila and thrust in their tops with a practiced motion of his thumb. 'Where is the water?'

'Do you really need some, Ranson?' Winter squatted on the floor and opened three of the cans.

'Yes. I'm thirsty, I didn't have anything to drink for two days remember.' He stared at the doctor. 'Why? Is anything wrong?'

'We didn't load much water, Ranson. We didn't have time.'

'I know that. It was the main reason why I left those people behind, but we had some water, a few gallons at least. Surely some must be left?'

'The tank developed a crack after takeoff,' said Winter quietly. 'We have exactly four pints of water left.'

'I see.' Tiredly, Ranson slumped against a bulkhead. 'Four pints, a day's supply, and we have at least three days' travel before we reach the Solar System.' He stared at the steaming container in his hand. 'Well, at least we have plenty of food and the soup may help stave off our thirst.'

'The soup has been vitaminised,' reminded Winter. 'If anything, it will increase, not quench, thirst.'

'To hell with it!' Ranson lifted his thermocan and drained the contents. 'I'm tired of worrying. If I'm going to die, then at least I'll die on a full stomach. He reached for a second container. 'Drink your soup. You're going to need all the energy you can get before we're through.'

Grimly he stared at the vibrating hyper-drive unit.

12

The phoney war

Gerald Lasser, Supreme Head of Armed Forces, sat in his office and listened to the quiet, respectful tones of the Emissary from Rigel. A big man, he showed the pink bloom of a man who used the gymnasium to keep his once-muscular body fit, and his smooth hair and enigmatic eyes gave him an air of spurious efficiency. Now he listened, his lips slightly pursed, his thick fingers toying with a stylo, as the thin man from Rigel X voiced his complaint,

'And so you see, Excellency. The position is serious. Rigel X is centred in a chlorine area and the Ginzoes are ruining our trade. I don't even know whether I will be able to escape their net and rejoin my family. It is essential that we have armed warships to protect us from the enemy.'

'Every planet thinks that they need armed warships,' Lasser's voice was deceptive, a deep, almost smug purr, a voice designed to hide the thoughts behind the words.

'We do not think, Excellency. We know!'

'Indeed?'

'Yes.' The Emissary thinned his lips as he thought of the people who had sent him to Earth. 'If I may remind your Excellency, our taxes more than cover the cost of maintaining such a vessel. We have paid these taxes for ten years now, and, though I do not feel that way myself, the people are beginning to wonder why they should pay money to Earth at all if they have no protection in return. I mention this because I have been so instructed. I have no personal doubt as to your strategy, you understand.'

'I understand.' Lasser nodded ponderously. 'In other words, unless you get what you want we get no more money. Is that it?'

'Well — '

'Fool!' The crash of Lasser's hand

thudding down on to his wide desk made the thin man start. 'Do you think Earth hasn't enough worries? Do you think that the strain of trying to protect every oxygen world in the galaxy is an easy one? Money, you say. But will money build ships? Will it replace the men who die so that your precious trade may continue?'

'I cannot be interested in that.' The thin man stirred uncomfortably in his chair. 'I am only the representative of my people, you understand. They have given me certain instructions.'

'Yes?'

'I have been informed to notify your Excellency that unless we receive armed protection from Terra, we will resign from the Federation and make our own peace with the enemy.' He fell silent, half-afraid of the effects of his words, half-relieved at having said them. Lasser nodded, and his eyes, as he stared at the Emissary seemed to be filled with pain.

'You will get your warship,' he said quietly. 'Even if I have to strip the Terran fleet, you will have your protection. I'd rather see Earth a shambles than have

Rigel X resign from the Federation.'

'But, Excellency — '

'Enough. You have made your threat. It would need only that, need only the example of one planet divorcing itself from the Federation, for others to follow your lead and destroy all we have worked for. Once the Federation is broken the enemy will move in and then what of your trade? It is only the constant threat of heavy reprisals that force the Ginzoes to leave our worlds alone. Once they learn that the Federation has been broken, that the overall strategy has been destroyed, they will blast the oxygen worlds as they will.'

'I did not mean that, Excellency, I — '

'The interview is over.' Lasser pressed a button on his desk. 'You will have your warship. That is all.'

He lifted his head as a small, somehow furtive man entered the room, and gestured towards the Emissary.

'Arrange for a Class Four warship to be sent to Rigel X. This gentleman will arrange billeting and supplies for the vessel.' He nodded towards the thin man.

'That is all. You will be notified when it is time to depart.'

'Thank you.' The Emissary bowed and left the room, almost running in his haste to escape the accusing eyes of the big man. Lasser watched him go with a silent contempt, then frowned as the furtive man gave a satisfied chuckle.

'Another one, Lasser. They beg for the ships and men to force them into bondage.'

'Need you say that, Quedron?'

'Why not?' Quedron sat on the edge of the wide desk. 'Don't make the one fatal mistake, Lasser. Don't ever begin believing your own publicity. At the moment you are Supreme Head, but you can be displaced tomorrow and thrown into the gutter.'

'You dare!' Anger made the big man tense and his eyes grew narrow and dangerous. 'Watch your tongue, man! I'm no tool to be used and thrown aside.'

'No?' The small man shrugged. 'Perhaps not. But no man is indispensable, Lasser. Especially when so many others depend on him.'

'The oxygen worlds depend on me, Quedron. What I do, I do for them. Once I have assembled a fleet large and strong enough to crush the Ginzoes, then the war will be over, but until then we must move slowly and carefully.'

'And in the meantime you sit pretty as Supreme Head. What were you before the war, Lasser? A Captain, wasn't it? A minor rank with no hope of advancement and the prospect of a small pension after twenty years of sterile service. That was your life. Then Terrans contacted the Ginzoes and things began to move. You were an ambitious man then, you are still, but you have changed from the fanatical Captain you once were. Now you have position, command, the respect of Earth. Just how far would you go to retain those things?'

'I saw the danger and took steps to safeguard the oxygen worlds.'

'Did you, Lasser? Didn't you ever wonder how it was that the path to power was made so easy? There were others above you, men with more right to sit in the chair you now occupy. They are gone now. Only you have the Supreme power. Only you are in a position to end the war.'

'That I will never do.' Lasser rose from his chair and paced the room. 'Terrans cannot live with the Ginzoes. At first I had hoped that we could make this a short war, that we could blast the enemy with our superior might. I was wrong. We had neglected our armed forces for too long, and when they were needed, they couldn't do what they had to do. Altair taught us that when we strike we must obliterate all the chlorine worlds at one blow. I have worked for that ever since I came into power. I shall always work for it.'

'An idealist.' Quedron shrugged, there was a sneer in his voice. 'Are you trying to convince yourself, Lasser? You must be. No intelligent man could believe for a moment that you are sincere.'

'Steady, Quedron,' warned the big man. 'Even though you may be the Head of Intelligence, yet you can be shot like any other man.'

'If I am shot,' said the small man coldly, 'you will be deposed within a single day. Don't be a fool, man! You know as well as I do that we cannot destroy the Ginzoes. Even if we could I would be against it. Think what would happen if we destroyed the enemy. You would be a hero — for a day. You would be given medals and praise — and then you would be forgotten. The Terran fleet would crumble for lack of funds. The military would sink back to what it was before we contacted the enemy. Would you like that, Lasser? Would you like to be Supreme Head of a dozen ships and a thousand men? Now you rule the galaxy, in fact, if not in name. Could you give up that power?'

'We must destroy the Ginzoes.'

'Why? What harm do they do? What harm can they cause?' Quedron twisted his lips in a cynical grin. 'They are the one thing you cannot do without, Lasser. Once you destroy them you destroy the very reason for your own existence. I thought you knew that.'

'I know it,' said the big man tiredly. 'I've heard all this before, but still it doesn't seem to make sense. We are at war and while we continue to be at war I have absolute power. I have ships and weapons and men. I have respect and the right of decision. I rule! And yet one thing bothers me, Quedron. I am a Terran and I must think of the Federation and the oxygen worlds. You say that we have no reason to fear the Ginzoes. I can't agree. What if they are preparing as we are preparing? What if they are only waiting for the one thing to give them absolute victory? What then?'

'Nothing.'

'What?'

'I said, nothing, and that is just what will happen. Why should they destroy us? They can't use our planets. They have no real reason to hate us. We have used them, Lasser. You know that better than anyone else. Alone you would still be a Captain, probably dead by now, forgotten. But a small group with foresight and ambition lifted you from that low rank and made you what you are. You cannot forget those men, Lasser. They made you — and they could break you.'

'Need you remind me of that?' Lasser

slumped into his chair. 'I know that I have been used. I know that the group you mentioned have made fortunes from the allocation of war contracts for ships and materials. I know, too, that they are the real rulers of Terra now. But never forget, Quedron, even a tool can grow tired of being used.'

'Meaning?'

'It is dangerous for any group to lift a man above their heads. History is full of examples of men who have burst their bonds and turned on those who helped them.'

'Perhaps.' Quedron shrugged, and his eyes, as he watched the restless movements of the big man held a secret amusement. 'But you will not turn on us. History can do more than teach, it can warn, and others can learn from what has happened in the past. You will do as you agreed. You will continue the phoney war, spreading armed warships over the galaxy, supposedly to guard the oxygen worlds, but in reality waiting to enforce our rule. Then, once the strategy is complete, you will remain in power, war or no war, and the military will come into their own again.'

'Yes,' breathed the big man, and his eyes glowed with fanatical ambition. 'We shall rule. The galaxy needs a strong man to guide its destiny. The Ginzoes have warned us of what we may expect in the future. When our hyper-drive ships finally make the Big Jump and cross the gulf between the galaxies, then we shall need the strong shield of military might to protect us from the ravages of other alien life forms.'

'Yes,' said Quedron quietly. 'The Ginzoes have warned us.'

'The Ginzoes!' Hate and anger made the big man's voice brittle and sharp. 'Scum! Crawling life fit only to die. There is no room in the universe for both aliens and men. We must crush them, Quedron. We must blast them from the surface of every chlorine world in the galaxy. Men cannot tolerate sharing their destiny with others.'

Quedron laughed.

He leaned back on the edge of the desk and his small body shook with genuine mirth. Lasser stared at the small man, and his broad features mottled with anger.

'Quedron!'

Still the laughter gushed from the furtive looking man, echoing flatly from the walls of the room, and whispering from the corners.

'Quedron! Stop it!'

'Sorry.' The small man gulped and wiped his eyes. 'You don't know how funny you sound, Lasser. Just like a hero on the tri-di screens. Man! Do you really believe all that guff?'

'I believe in the destiny of the oxygen worlds!'

'Sure you do. We all do, but not the same way as you. I warned you about starting to believe your own publicity.'

'What do you mean?'

'You hate the Ginzoes, don't you, Lasser? You've never even done more than glance at one, never spoken to one, never tried to find out what makes them tick. But you hate them. You hate them because they aren't men.'

'Isn't that reason enough?'

'For you — perhaps. For others — no! The Ginzoes are useful, Lasser. Too useful for you to be permitted to upset everything by your illogical hate. You don't know it yet, but you're going to have reason to thank them on your bended knees. When we've finally given you the galaxy on a platter, remember it was the Ginzoes who made it possible.'

'I don't understand you? What are you driving at?'

'Have you seen Warren lately?' The small man grinned as he asked the question. Lasser frowned and shook his head.

'No. Not for several weeks now. Why?'

'He's gone to fix up a deal with the Ginzoes.' Quedron chuckled at the expression on the big man's face. 'We guessed that you'd feel like the way you do and so we had to keep it a secret until it was all over. This war is going to stop. Really stop, I mean, but naturally, we'll still continue to frighten the people and collect their taxes. We can use every ship and man we can get.'

'But why? If the war is to stop, and I

don't agree with that for one moment, the people will get to know about it. Why should they pay taxes then?'

'Because if they refuse there won't be any more people.' Quedron smiled at the blank expression in the other's eyes. 'I'm saving all the details until Warren returns. He should be here any day now, he should have arrived days ago, and when he does — ' The small man drew a deep breath. 'We'll share the galaxy between us!'

'Why wasn't I informed about this?' Lasser glared at the small man. 'How dared you think of making a deal with the enemies of Terra? What was this deal, anyway?'

'Never mind about that now. You'll know all about it when you have to, not before. I'm waiting for Warren, he had the idea and he was the one to carry it through.'

'But I must know!'

'Must you?' Quedron slipped from the edge of the desk and moved easily towards the door. 'Stick to your toys, Lasser. Stay with your ships and guns and men dressed in pretty uniforms. Leave the real work, the brainwork, to those who have something inside their skulls except clichés and outworn metaphors. You do as you are told and don't bother to think about it, I'm offering you a share of the galaxy. I'm offering you absolute rule, despotic power, and you want to argue about it. What do you care how it was done? What did you care about continuing the phoney war? You wanted power, didn't you? Well, you have it. You want to remain in power, don't you? Then leave it to those who know more about such things than you will ever know.'

He paused by the door and looked back at the big man.

'The galaxy, Lasser. On a platter.'

Softly the door swung shut behind him, the thick panel cutting off all external noise. Lasser stared at it, his broad features set and cold, his blood churning through his tormented brain.

Quedron was right!

The small man had spoken the truth — and that was the pity of it. He did want power. He did want the feeling of respect and absolute rule. He had imagined at first that it was his own genius that had raised him so high, so fast, then, when he learned the bitter truth, he had continued to deny it even to himself.

But now he could deny it no longer.

Warren had made a deal with the enemy. One of the cabal had made a pact with the Ginzoes. Lasser frowned as he wondered what that pact could have been. He hadn't been consulted. He had been ignored and that fact warned him just what to expect from his allies. They would use him to the last, and then they would eliminate him.

A thin smile twisted the lips of the big man. An animal, tiger-like snarl of soundless fury, and one of his hands clenched, closing into a rock-hard fist.

He was thinking of Warren.

13

Return to Earth

They emerged within ten million miles of Earth. They broke from hyperspace with a screaming whine from the overstrained hyper-drive, and within minutes they were ringed by armed patrol vessels and the ether was alive with pulsing radio messages.

Ranson sat in his chair and stared at the flickering surface of the visi-screen.

He was filthy, his features dabbled with blood, his skin grimed with dirt, his hair and beard a tangled, redolent mass. He sagged in the padded chair, his red-rimmed eyes dull as they stared at the visi-screen, and, for a long time he paid no attention to the shrilling alarm from the radio. Then, moving as an old man might move, he threw the toggle and listened to the crisp voice vibrating from the speaker.

'Patrol ship XSE 243. Identify your-selves.'

Ranson parted his cracked and swollen lips and croaked a few words.

'What?' The patrol officer sounded annoyed. 'Speak up! Identify yourselves, or I fire!'

'Emergency,' whispered Ranson. He swallowed and wetted his lips with the contents of a thermocan. 'Emergency!'

'What is the nature of your emergency? Where are you from?'

'Damn you!' Ranson shuddered to the sound of his own voice. 'We're dying in here. No water. Hyper-drive vibrating in the ultrasonic. Emergency. Blast your eyes! Bring water: For God's sake bring water!'

'Where are you from?' The speaker rattled the question and Ranson snarled at it with soundless hate.

'What the hell does it matter where we're from? We're dying, I tell you. Send a doctor and water. Your damn questions can wait, but we can't. I — ' He slumped as the fury of his anger died and weakness reclaimed his tormented body. He groaned, his grey, blood-shot eyes staring vacantly at the dull surface of the visi-screen, and his mind refusing to make sense of the words rattling from the radio.

After what seemed a long time the chattering ceased, continued again, then fell silent. Sounds echoed through the ship, the metallic sounds of the air lock being opened and booted feet clumping into the ship and ringing from the deck plates.

A man stood over Ranson.

He was tall, sealed in a lightweight-spacesuit, and, on his breast and helmet the red cross on a white circle denoted his medical profession.

'Here!' The word vibrated from the diaphragm set into the helmet, and Ranson gasped as a cold spray, wetted his face.

'Water!' He reached for the pressure-tank and the doctor gently pushed him back into the pilot's chair.

'Take it easy. What's wrong? Disease?'

'No.' The young commander opened his mouth, trying to ease his parched throat with the chilly water. 'We lost our water. The hyper-drive began vibrating in the ultrasonic and we daren't emerge because it wouldn't have started again.' He reached for the water, and this time the doctor allowed him to swallow a little.

'How long?'

'I'm not certain. We should have made it in three days, but it was longer than that. I've not had water for five days now, just soup from the thermocans.' Ranson gulped and shivered to the mind-clearing spray of icy water. 'I'd guess seven days.'

'You look it.' The doctor glanced towards the companionway as another medical officer entered the control room.

'Well?'

'They'll live. Two men and a girl. No signs of disease, but they are all in. No water and little food. They all bear traces of ultrasonic disruption and the girl is suffering from space fever. Harmless though, just the normal radiation temperature rise most people get first time in space.'

'Good. Radio for the personnel carriers. These people must get to hospital and the sooner the better.'

'Hospital?' Ranson jerked himself upright in his chair. 'No. Put me in contact with Lasser. I've got to speak to Lasser. I — ' He sagged, his emaciated body collapsing in the padded chair, and the doctor shrugged.

'Poor devil. Advanced dehydration and surface deterioration. Might be some cerebral haemorrhage and internal lesions. In any case, we'll have to watch him over the quarantine regulations.'

Impatiently he gestured towards the men bearing the coffin-like, airtight, space stretcher.

Six days later they sat before the investigation officer of the Terran fleet.

Ranson glared at the young captain, almost writhing with impatience on the hard chair. Next to him, Handley knotted his big fists, and Winter and the girl sat and waited for the endless delays and questions to cease.

'You state that you came from the Altair sector.' The captain glanced at his papers. 'Examination of your vessel shows that it has rested for many years on an oxygen world. There are traces of molds and bacteria, you understand.'

'How many times must I tell you what happened?' Ranson half-rose from his chair, then slumped back at a curt gesture. 'We found the ship on a backwoods planet. The Ginzoes dropped us there after taking us from my own ship. Damn it, man, I was cleared from Earth! You have only to look up the papers.'

'That has been done,' said the captain stiffly. 'You cleared for Deneb IV with one passenger, a Mr. Warren. Where is he now?'

'Dead. I told you that my ship was caught by a Ginzo patrol. They blasted us with their vortex guns and we drifted for days before they took us off.'

'Why did they rescue you?'

'I don't know. I don't think that they suspected we were alive. They wanted the hyper-drive unit and boarded us to cut it free.'

'Then your passenger was killed during action?'

'No. He died while on the Ginzo ship.'

'I see.' The young officer frowned. 'You admit then, that you were with the enemy for many days?'

'Of course I admit it!' Ranson jerked to his feet and began striding about the room. 'Look,' he said tensely, 'I've told you all this before. For Heaven's sake let me speak to Lasser. All this is just wasting time.'

'Is it?' The captain shrugged. 'Perhaps you would like us to ignore the safety regulations? Perhaps you would like us to leave Earth defenceless against alien disease or enemy spies?'

'Are we diseased?' Ranson glared at the officer. 'They've kept us in that hospital for six days now. We're clean, and you know it. Why are you keeping us here? You've checked our story, you've examined our ship, and you've even tested our body molds. Doesn't all that satisfy you? What more can we do to prove to you that we aren't spies?'

'You can cooperate!' The officer glared at the young commander and gestured towards the chair. 'Now, sit down.' He waited until Ranson had slumped down onto the hard chair. 'We have tested you,' he said quietly, 'and you are free from infection. We have also examined your vessel.' He paused, staring at the silent commander. 'How is it that you have an alien compound daubed on your hull? A compound that our chemists state could only originate on a chlorine world. How do you explain that?'

'The Ginzoes did it. They marked the hull so that we wouldn't be fired on by their patrols.'

'Indeed? And why?'

'Because we carry a message from them to Lasser.'

'And the message?'

'Will be told to Lasser only.' Ranson thinned his lips as he stared at the young officer. 'The quicker you get us to the Supreme Head the better. If it is any consolation to you I can tell you this. Lasser will promote you for using your head and taking me to him. If you insist on being a fool, you will die.'

'So now you threaten me.' The captain smiled as he reached into a drawer and produced a high velocity pistol. 'Such talk makes me more suspicious of you than ever. How do I know that you haven't been primed by the Ginzoes? They could have hypnotized you, given you a post hypnotic command to kill the Supreme Head as soon as you saw him, a command which you wouldn't even know you had. No. I think it better to have you thoroughly cleared first.'

'How long will that take?'

'A few days. Perhaps even a week. We must be sure, you understand.'

'Within a week you'll be as good as dead.' Ranson wiped at the sweat glistening on his forehead. 'Can't you cut all this red tape? All I ask is an audience with Lasser. Ten minutes would do. Five even, but I must have it now. A week will be too late. Damn it, man, I've been a prisoner of the Ginzoes. Doesn't that earn me a few minutes with the man who is fighting them?'

'Certainly. And you'll get it — after you're cleared.'

'You're determined not to use your intelligence, aren't you?' Ranson leaned forward and glared into the officer's eyes. 'You intend sitting here, protected by your red tape, operating strictly according to regulations. And all the time you wait here the Ginzo ships are getting nearer, and nearer, and nearer — His voice died into silence, then he leaned back and smiled, metal gleaming from one hand.

'Stay where you are, Captain. Move, and I'll use this toy on you. It's yours, so you should know whether or not it's loaded. Well?'

'You — ' Anger twisted the features of the officer. He stared at the gun as if stupefied, and Ranson smiled, a cold smile without the slightest trace of humour.

'I took it,' he said gently. 'I took it while your attention was diverted, while you stared into my eyes. Remember that on another occasion. Remember that the only time to show a weapon is when you intend using it.' His voice hardened as he rose to his feet. 'Now! Take me to Lasser!'

'I refuse.' The officer swallowed and tried to look defiant. 'You can't make me do anything.'

'Can't I?' Ranson swung the pistol with blinding speed and savage violence, and the officer whimpered as the metal smashed against his cheek. 'You refuse?'

Again the pistol swept towards the pale features of the young officer and blood spurted from his pulped nose. 'Do I beat your face to a jelly or do you take me to Lasser?' Again the weapon swung towards the blood-streaked face of the captain, and he screamed, lifting his hands to ward off the blow.

'Stop! Stop it, I tell you!'

'Handley. Search the desk, look for another pistol.' Ranson stared down at the officer, not troubling to disguise his contempt. 'You're going to take me to Lasser. You're soft and unused to violence, proud and vain of your good looks. You'd do anything rather than suffer pain. Now. Either you do as I order or I'll smash your face into bloody pulp! Well?' He lifted the pistol, and the officer cowered deep in his padded chair.

'No!'

'Right. You asked for it!' Ranson's lips thinned to a cruel line as he brought down the pistol.

'I'll do it! Don't hurt me again! I'll do it!'

Ranson drew back his arm as the

captain babbled the words and the slender barrel of the pistol whined through the air just before his starting eyes.

'Good. Now, where is he? How do I get to him?' Impatiently he dragged the officer from his chair. 'Talk, damn you! Talk fast!'

'He's in his office. Top of the building. There is a direct elevator at the end of the corridor.' The captain whimpered as he saw the blood dripping from his broken nose. Ranson grunted, and his closed fist moved in a short and vicious arc, the sound of its impact sounding strangely loud in the soundproofed room. Deliberately he let the unconscious body of the officer fall to the floor.

'Did you find anything, Handley?'

'No. He only had the one gun.'

'Then let's go. Down the corridor and up the elevator. There may be guards, but if there are, leave them to Handley and me.' He stared at Winter, and the pale face of the girl. 'One of us must get to Lasser and give him the message. *Must!* Unless peace is declared within three days it will be too late. Remember that, and remember that we aren't worrying about the lives of anyone who gets in our way. We are trying to save the lives of half the galaxy, every man and woman on every oxygen world in the universe.'

He stared at them for a long moment, then, moving with a quick, nervous impatience, he opened the door and stepped into the passage.

Ahead of them waited the elevator.

Tensely they walked towards the waiting cage, Ranson in the lead, then Winter and the girl, with the big engineer following last. The sound of their footsteps echoed softly from the walls, and every moment the young commander expected the challenge of a guard.

None came. They reached the elevator, pressed the signal button, then waited, nerves jumping, for the automatic doors to hiss open.

'I don't like this.' Handley stared into the bare interior of the elevator. 'Where is everyone? This place should be full of guards.'

'I don't know.' Ranson frowned as he

stepped into the elevator. 'It might be luck, we could use some after what we've been through. Anyway, we can't stay here. That stupid officer will be screaming for help soon, and they'll search the building with orders to shoot on sight.' He stabbed his thumb at the topmost button. 'Let's hope that Lasser is alone and in a good mood.'

Delila groaned as the thrust of the cage reminded her of the agony of takeoff, and Ranson smiled at her, and squeezed her arm. 'Scared?'

'A little.' She swallowed and looked at him with a peculiar expression. 'Did you have to hit that officer?'

'The captain?' Ranson shrugged. 'Don't give it a second thought. If anything it will do him good. Maybe he'll recognise sincerity the next time he meets up with it.' He looked at her, frowning a little at her expression. 'What's the matter?'

'You look good without whiskers,' she said abruptly, and blushed. 'I thought you were a lot older than you are.'

'What?' Ranson stared at her, then at Winter's ironical grin, and shrugged.

Tension caused people to act in peculiar ways, and he guessed that her remark was caused by reaction. He fingered his shaven chin and cropped hair, savouring the cleanliness after weeks of unshaven dirt. Handley's voice echoed in the tiny cage.

'What if Lasser doesn't believe us, Carl?'

'He'll believe us,' said the young commander grimly. 'I'll see to that.'

'By beating his face in?' Delila glared her contempt, and Ranson stared at her, startled by the sudden change in her voice and expression.

'Yes,' he said drily. 'If necessary. The fate of the oxygen worlds is more important than personal squeamishness.'

'Must you be so brutal?'

'Am I?' He shrugged. 'Perhaps you would rather I sat down and just let the Ginzoes destroy our worlds. It isn't easy to beat a man to a jelly, Delila. It wasn't easy to abandon those people to the fanatical colonists on your own planet. It wasn't easy, but it had to be done. Do you want me to give up now? Do you want to see the oxygen worlds transformed into chlorine ones?'

'They wouldn't dare do that.'

'No? You have a right to your own opinion but personally I'd feel a lot safer if peace were declared. You forget, I've seen the Ginzoes and talked with them. You haven't.'

'They could be bluffing,' said Handley slowly. 'We could have been taken in by Warren's talk. After all, we can't be certain that he did actually give them the catalyst.'

'I know that. They could have fixed the demonstration between Warren's death and their arrival in the cell. I've been wondering about the time lag. They had plenty of time to stop what happened if they had wanted to. Warren was yelling for help for a long while before he finally died.'

'Maybe they didn't want him to live. Maybe that's why they gave him an empty flare-gun.'

'Maybe a lot of things, Handley. Maybe they are bluffing. Maybe the catalyst doesn't exist — but we can't be sure. We can never be sure, and so — ' He hefted the slender bulk of the high velocity pistol. 'Lasser must be persuaded to declare peace.'

Softly the elevator slowed to a halt. The doors hissed open, operated by their automatic relays, and brilliant light shone through the widening gap.

Light — and the menacing orifices of levelled guns!

14

Lasser decides

There were three of them, three long barrelled high velocity rifles, and Ranson stared at them, narrowing his eyes against the glare of the too-bright light. For a moment no one moved, then, speaking from behind the guards, a small, furtive looking man rapped quick orders.

'Come out with your hands raised. Quick now!'

Ranson hesitated, poising the pistol in his hand, judging his chances against the waiting guards. The small man chuckled, almost as if he were enjoying a huge joke

'Try it,' he urged. 'You might get one, maybe two, of the guards, but you'd never get all three. Those rifles are set for full automatic, by the way. One burst and the entire elevator would be riddled with HV slugs. I leave it to your imagination as to what would happen to your friends.' His voice hardened, lost its humour and became cruel. 'Throw out your gun. Raise your arms and step out of the cage. Quick now!'

Ranson shrugged and threw the pistol to the soft carpeting of the floor. Grimly he raised his arms, and, followed by the others, stepped out of the small cage.

'That's better.' The small man gestured towards a wide table. 'Now we can talk in comfort. So much better than chasing you all over the building, wasn't it? Naturally I know all about you, the officer had the sense to record your entire conversation. You owe your lives to the fact that you did not tell him the message you carry. What is it?'

'Where is Lasser?'

'The Supreme Head?' The small man shrugged. 'You can give me the message. I am Quedron, Head of Intelligence. I am to be trusted.'

'Are you?' Ranson glanced at the watchful guards. 'Are they? My business is with Lasser. I have come a long way to give him the message. I can go a little further.'

'How much further?'

'To the other room, shall we say? Is Lasser in there?'

'Yes.'

'Then shall we join him?'

'A moment.' Quedron whispered swift orders to the guards, and they saluted, turned on their heels, and left the room. Softly the small man crossed towards the wide table. 'Shall we sit?'

'Where is Lasser?'

'He will be here, but first I must know the nature of your message.' Quedron stared at the young commander. 'You were chartered by Warren to take him to Deneb IV. You said that you were blasted by the Ginzoes, and that Warren had died. Is that the fact?'

'Yes.'

'Did he say anything before he died?'

'Perhaps.' Ranson stared coldly at the small man. 'I told you that my message is for Lasser. You are wasting your time.'

'Then we shall call Lasser.' Irritably Quedron pressed a button and a door swung open. A guard glanced into the room and stiffened as he saw the small man.

'Call the Supreme Head,' ordered Quedron coldly. 'Then leave us.'

'Yes, sir.' The guard saluted again, and Ranson thinned his lips with sudden suspicion as he stared at the furtive figure of the Head of Intelligence. He was still staring when Lasser entered the room.

The big man seemed tired, his broad shoulders sagged with weariness and his heavy features were lined and haggard. He nodded to Quedron and stared dully at the four people sitting at the table.

'You wanted me?'

'Yes, Lasser.' Quedron pointed towards the young commander. 'This man has a message for you. A very important message. So important that he will tell it to no one else.' He chuckled again, enjoying his secret humour, and Lasser flushed.

'Well?' He slumped into a chair and glared at the young commander. 'What is it?'

'Simply this.' Ranson was surprised to find that his hands trembled and that his face was damp with perspiration. 'You have three days to declare peace and end the Ginzo war.'

'What! Are you insane?' Lasser half-rose from his chair and glared at the young man. 'Is this your idea of a stupid joke?'

'It's no joke,' snapped Ranson. 'Unless you declare peace the Ginzoes will destroy every oxygen world in the galaxy. They have a catalyst, a thing capable of breaking down sodium chloride into its basic elements. Dropped into the ocean it will liberate free chlorine and poison every living thing on the planet. You should know about it. It was one of your friends who gave it to the enemy. Warren. You know him?'

'Yes,' said Lasser heavily. 'I know him.' He slumped down into his chair and his eyes were dull as he stared at the small man. 'Was this the secret you were keeping from me?'

'No,' Quedron smiled. 'Warren had a wild idea, I told you that, but this man has the message all wrong. The Ginzoes won't harm us. Not until we give them orders to use their weapon. That was the pact Warren made with them. I promised you the galaxy on a platter, Lasser. Well, this is it. Now we can drop the mask. Now we can rule.'

'You fool!' Ranson stared at the small man. 'Do you really believe that the Ginzoes will put you in supreme power? Why should they?'

'Warren could answer that. He made the pact. Supreme power upheld by the Ginzo threat of destruction.'

'Warren is dead,' said Ranson tightly. 'He died screaming for help and threatening us with terrible death. The Ginzoes could have helped him, they could have saved his life, but they left him alone, Quedron, and now he is dead.'

'We can manage without him,' said the small man coldly. 'Warren was in many ways a fool.'

'You still don't understand what I am saying, do you, Quedron?' Ranson leaned across the wide table. 'Warren made a pact with the Ginzoes. He thought they had agreed to save his life, but when he called to them, when he felt hands around his throat and knew that he was going to die, they let him down. They could have saved him. They could have stopped what happened. They didn't, and Warren died.'

'You killed him.' It was a statement, not a question, and Ranson nodded.

'We killed him.'

'So!' Quedron smiled thinly. 'You know the penalty for murder? A lifetime of forced labour on Mercury. A lifetime! Naturally, with conditions there as they are a lifetime isn't very long. I understand that the prisoners are rather glad of that fact.'

'What sort of a man are you?' Ranson stared at Quedron, and shook his head. 'You still haven't understood what I am trying to tell you. Warren made a pact with the Ginzoes. A pact to save his life. He called to them for help — and they let him down! They let him die, Quedron. They broke their word. Now, can you still trust them to do as you wish?'

'No.' Lasser stirred in his chair and glared at the small man as he spoke. 'I knew nothing of this. I guessed something was happening, but not this. Why didn't you tell me, Quedron? Only a fool would imagine that the road to power lay in giving a knife to your enemy. What of the oxygen worlds? What of all the people who have trusted us? How can I face them now?'

'How?' Quedron shrugged. 'That is your worry, Lasser. You have played a game for ten years now, it shouldn't be hard to continue deceiving them. What are we doing but what has already been done? The war will end — and we shall rule. It is as simple as that.'

'No.' Lasser rose to his feet, and a pistol glinted in his hand. 'The war will not end. I will never agree to yield to the aliens. The War cannot end until every last one of them is smouldering ash.'

'Put away that toy, Lasser,' snapped the small man contemptuously. 'You wouldn't dare to kill me. You know too well what would happen if you did.'

For a moment the big man stared down at the Head of Intelligence, then, with a strangled sound coming from deep within his chest, threw the pistol on to the table.

'Damn you, Quedron! Damn you!'

'Damn me if you like, Lasser, but you will do as you are told. This war will end. We shall take supreme power, and the

Ginzoes will provide the constant threat necessary to bring the worlds to heel.'

'But what of the catalyst?' Ranson felt the engineer press against him as he leaned across the table. 'Did Warren really have such a thing?'

'Does it matter?' Quedron shrugged. 'The end result will be the same. As long as the people believe that the Ginzoes have the power to destroy their worlds they will toe the line. We can milk them dry, make them accept any conditions, make them only too pleased to accept us. It isn't really important at all. The threat will be enough.'

'But what of the declaration of peace? Once the war is officially over the people will never agree to support the Terran fleet.'

'Naturally, the war will not be over — officially. We will be at peace with the Ginzoes but it will be a secret peace. The people must still believe that we are protecting them from their enemies. At least for long enough to ensure that we are firmly in power.'

'We have three days,' reminded Ranson

grimly. 'Three days to radio a full declaration of peace to all the galaxy.'

'Nonsense! They must wait a few years. A galaxy can't be won in a few days.'

'We have three days,' repeated Ranson, and suddenly Quedron lost his contemptuous smile.

'Put down that gun!'

'No.' Ranson hefted the slender bulk of the high velocity pistol that Lasser had thrown on to the table. 'Peace will be declared within three days. You will agree — or you will die!'

'You think so?' Quedron leaned back in his chair. 'I should warn you that this room is covered by the weapons of my guards. Kill me and you die, all of you. Now. Drop that pistol and listen to reason. Drop it, I say!'

'No.' Lasser rose from his chair and towered over the small man. 'Listen to me, Quedron. I've taken orders from you for long enough. I've agreed to them because, in a way, you offered me what I wanted. I thought that I could use you as you were using me, I hoped that once I had built a large enough fleet I could destroy the Ginzoes and end this war with honour. Now I know I can't do that. Now you sit there and tell me that you have sold us out. That you have betrayed everything I've ever worked for, hoped for, longed for. But one thing I can tell you, Quedron. There will be no peace with the aliens, secret or otherwise!'

'Don't be a fool, Lasser! Stand out of the line of fire!' Ranson surged forward and the muzzle of his weapon gouged into the small man's throat. 'That's better. Now call to your guards, Quedron. Call to them — and we'll all die together!'

'What do you want?' Quedron twisted his head as he tried to draw away from the thrusting pistol.

'I want a declaration of peace radioed throughout the galaxy by hyper-beam radio. And I want it done now. Lasser! Get to the intercom and arrange for a priority broadcast. Quick, man! Hurry!'

'There will be no peace.' Lasser thinned his lips with determination. 'I will not yield to the aliens.'

'Fool! Why not? Do you want to see the oxygen worlds destroyed?'

'We can guard our planets. I will not yield to aliens.'

'Guard the planets? How many and with what?' Ranson drew back his teeth in an animal-snarl. 'Damn you, Lasser! You will do as I say. This war was born in fear, continued through greed, and it will end in destruction if you don't do as I say. What do I care for honour? What does your petty ambition mean to the billions of men and women scattered throughout the galaxy? You are one man, Lasser. One weak, ambitious fool, but you are the only man who can declare peace within the stated period. Do it, man. Do it now!'

'No.'

'Why not? Is it because the aliens aren't men? Is it because you are too blind to recognise that intelligence isn't a monopoly of Earth? The Ginzoes are different from us in many ways, but in one way we are brothers. We both have the gift of intelligence and the ability to reason. They have warned us to stop this stupid conflict. They are testing us, Lasser, and they have the means to destroy us if we show our lack of common logic. Damn it, man! We have no choice! Unless you declare peace we shall die. All of us! Is that worth your petty pride?'

'They could be bluffing,' said the big man slowly. 'The Ginzoes might just be forcing us to stop the war because they feel that we are winning.'

'Are we?' Ranson shook his head. 'I doubt it. They could be bluffing. I have thought of that, but, can we ever be certain one way or the other? Is it worth the risk? Once the oceans have been seeded the end is inevitable. Dare we take that gamble?'

'We could attack. We could destroy some of their worlds.'

'And in return they would render the oxygen worlds unfit for human life. They wouldn't lose a thing, Lasser. All they need to do is to wait a few years and then take over our planets. We can't do that. We can't breathe chlorine.' He stared at the big man and his eyes narrowed with sudden impatience. 'Well?'

'I — '

'I'll settle it for you, then.' Savagely he dug the pistol into Quedron's throat.

'Unless you agree I'll kill this man. Then, unless his guards kill us all, I'll kill you. I mean it, Lasser. I've done too much and come too far to be stopped now. If you refuse to save the galaxy, you die. Well?'

Lasser hesitated, staring at the congested features of the small man, then, slowly, his eyes moved down the wide table. Winter stared at him, Handley, and the smooth face of the girl tensed with the effort of remaining silent,

'I mean it, Lasser.' Ranson stared at the big man. 'What is your life to me? I'll kill you even though we all die for it. One thing is certain, you will never regret not declaring peace — you won't live long enough. Well?'

'I — ' Lasser swallowed, great beads of sweat glistening on his features, 'I agree!'

'Good!' Ranson jerked his head towards the inner room. 'Let's all go in there now. Let me hear you give the orders.'

'Don't you trust me?'

'I trust you,' said the young commander grimly. 'I don't think that you could be fool enough or criminal enough to place your own desires above the oxygen worlds. But there are others, men like Warren and Quedron here. It would be better if you disposed of them, Lasser. Much better!'

'Yes,' said the big man, and Quedron snarled at the expression in his eyes. 'Once peace is declared I won't need them. I shall still be Supreme Head of Armed Forces. I shall still have my ships and my men. What do I want with Galactic Rule? I am a soldier and I have work to do.' He smiled and turned to the intercom. 'Operator. Arrange galactic wide hookup on hyper-beam. I have a message of tremendous importance to the peoples of the Federation of Man.' His voice droned on as he recorded the peace declaration, and Ranson sighed as he released his grip on the small man.

'What made him change his mind, Carl?' Handley frowned at the big man standing before the transmitter. Ranson shrugged.

'Lasser hated the aliens. He didn't know why, but really that hate was a projection of his own dislike of what he was and what he was doing. He couldn't hurt himself. He couldn't hurt his allies, the men who were using him to further their own ambition, so he vented his rage on the Ginzoes. I broke that vicious circle. I forced him to alter his viewpoint. Now, though he doesn't love the Ginzoes, he has lost his insane hatred of them.' He glanced at the small man. 'I wouldn't like to be in his friend's shoes now,' he said slowly. 'Lasser is still Supreme Head and he may do something about all the insults he has had to bear and all the orders he has had to take. He has resolved his own ambitions now, Quedron. He knows what he wants — and it doesn't include galactic domination.'

He smiled as Delila crossed the room towards him.

'Is it all over now, Carl?'

'Yes, Delila. I'll get a new ship, probably Lasser will let me have one of the surplus fleet now, and take you back home.' He glanced at the big engineer. 'You know, Handley,' he said slowly. 'One thing worries me. Were the Ginzoes bluffing? Did they really have the catalyst, or did they just take advantage of an opportunity to end the war?'

'I don't know, Carl. We shall never know. But does it matter?'

'No,' said the young commander, and smiled down at the woman by his side. 'It doesn't matter at all — now!'

Delila blushed.

THE END

We do hope that you have enjoyed reading this large print book.

Did you know that all of our titles are available for purchase?

We publish a wide range of high quality large print books including:
Romances, Mysteries, Classics
General Fiction
Non Fiction and Westerns

Special interest titles available in large print are:
The Little Oxford Dictionary
Music Book, Song Book
Hymn Book, Service Book

Also available from us courtesy of Oxford University Press:
Young Readers' Dictionary
(large print edition)
Young Readers' Thesaurus
(large print edition)

For further information or a free brochure, please contact us at:
Ulverscroft Large Print Books Ltd.,
The Green, Bradgate Road, Anstey,
Leicester, LE7 7FU, England.
Tel: (00 44) **0116 236 4325**
Fax: (00 44) **0116 234 0205**

THE MULTI-MAN

John Russell Fearn

Research biologist Jeffrey Dexter's experiments produce a creature capable of endless reproduction, yet lacking human reserve. Then he's murdered — swept aside by the ruthless Multi-Man. Dexter's wife's claim, that the new Jeffrey Dexter is only a cellular duplicate of her husband, finds her incarcerated in an institution for the mentally unbalanced. Dexter No 2 develops his plans: famous people are duplicated to nominate Dexter's Presidency in a new scientific era. Can Scotland Yard Detective Sergeant Hanbuy hold him back?

MAKE IT NYLONS

Gordon Landsborough

Joe P. Heggy, professional trouble-buster for an international construction firm, is travelling to Turkey. As the plane lands in Istanbul he looks out of the window and witnesses a murder — a man being stabbed. The victim was the leader of the country's Ultra-Nationalist Party. That glimpse of murder brings him trouble. Millions of fanatics try to pin the crime on him — his life is in danger. His only ally — an Amazonian Rumanian peasant with a passion for western nylons!

THE PREDATORS

Sydney J. Bounds

Following years of hard training, Lee Sabre graduates as a Predator, First Class — an instrument of the Galactic Federation, which has conquered and subjugated his homeworld of Terra — once known as the Earth. The Federation sends Sabre and his team on their first space mission, where he is approached by the Terran Underground, an organisation determined to overthrow their alien yoke . . . and his decision could have a devastating effect on millions of lives, and the existence of Earth itself.